THE VIOLET HOUR

BRYNN CHAPMAN

.

The Violet Hour
Copyright © 2015 by R. R. Hochbein

Produced in the United States of America, all rights reserved.

Publisher: R. R. Hochbein

For Cade

#YouAreMySunshine
#ThanksForBeingMyLight

Lost Time is never found again.
~Benjamin Franklin

Some people die at twenty and five, but aren't
buried till seventy-five.
~Benjamin Franklin

PROLOGUE

1859 Charleston, South Carolina
Seaside~The Opera House

If you are doing this. It must be now.

The blood-red opera-house curtains undulate, a mere six inches from the chair on which I sit.

If I move my boot forward, extend my leg a meager inch, my toe would poke from beneath them—visible to the nearly three hundred townsfolk gathered behind it.

"We are thrilled and pleased—"

Rivulets of sweat snake down my neck, running into my dress. My hands are clammy and I readjust my violin. It slides down to the frets and I nearly drop it.

My heartbeat doubles and a wave of fear pulses. *It must be now—It must be now.*

"Her name is oft used in company with the words, virtuoso. Perfect pitch."

I cock my head and *hear it*. The surf *pounding* the shore, just outside the window.

Images flash.

Her lithe body, bloated and purple, bobbing beneath the waves in a whirling tornado of tiny bubbles.

I clamp my eyes together.

Another flash.

The empty coffin. Oh dear heaven sustain me the empty coffin.

I stand. Am walking, not seeing. I clutch the violin to my chest. I stumble toward my dressing room. It is my imagination, of course. They never found her body.

"She has toured the halls of Europe, Asia, and is now here, once again, to grace our lovely Charleston stage."

I fling open the door, grasp a calling card and scribble on the back of it. I ring the bell and fling a few day dresses into my bag.

The servant appears; her black eyes wide and afraid. I thrust some coins into her outstretched palm, along with a note. "This is for Sarah. Do you understand me? Sarah only."

She shakes her head *no*, clearly terrified. I drop two more in. "Sarah. Go now!"

I spin her—shoving her back out the stage door. I insist on utter solitude prior to performing. But it shan't last. Right outside the thin wooden door lurk opportunists, fans, soliders…*him.*

I stride forward, the room tilts and obscures, so that all in my focus is the window. The low-enough-to-the-ground escape route.

I sling my leg out the ledge and as my head pokes out, the surf roars louder, conjuring more images.

2

No, No, NO. Do not think on her. Do not think on her.

I *jump.* Leap from the ledge and crumple to the damp earth; the strong smell of the sea invading my nostrils as they flare. Resurrection fern blowing in the soft air of dusk.

My ankles wail as I scramble to stand.

Charleston is alive and bustling despite the darkening hour.

I stride forward into the crowd, ripping off my wig, my wincing at the hot pain in my scalp as the pins pull free—and fling it beneath a bougainvillea bush.

I lurch into the crowd, and am instantly swallowed.

The smell of Charleston sweet-grass fills my nostrils. Our last visit, my mother fingering the weaving of the sweet-grass baskets, deciding which to buy.

I tilt my chin higher. I must appear brave. Blend into the throng if I have any chance of escape.

I have rehearsed this countless times in my mind. My stomach lurches with fear and I swallow down the bile that threatens.

Applause erupts in *The Seaside*, wafting down onto the crowds through the myriad of open windows.

Sweat breaks under my arms, on my forehead. I hurry forward, forcing myself not to run. Look forward, do not meet their gazes.

I hear the crowd's murmuring confusion, growing louder and louder, till the manager takes the stage once again. The recommencing of the orchestra. Hissess and boo's.

Gooseflesh erupts from nape to bottom. He will *flay me*. Flay me alive.

Behind, just within earshot, the opera house door bangs open and I flinch. "Where are you? Come back this instant, I say!"

A man collides with my shoulder and I feel something *thud* against my shoulder, bouncing to the ground. My eyes dart frantically, trying to locate it through the myriad of boots.

No. No. It is all that remains of her. I quickly finger my other ear, wrenching the remaining earring from it, shoving it to safety within the secret pocket in my skirt.

"*Where are you?*" His deranged voice rings out over the crowd, and many stop to stare at his beet-red face.

I see her then. Her tall, red head sticking up above the crowd. She's poised by a hansom; her hand on the door..

She sees me coming and flings it wide and crawls inside.

I hurtle in, slamming the door.

Sarah bangs the side of the carriage. "Drive on!"

Sarah's grasp is a hot-vice; despite her glove I feel the perspiration beneath. She bites her full lip, trying to be brave. She has no tears, thank heaven, or I might disintegrate myself.

"It is fine. The day has finally arrived," I speak quietly, even though the only chance of an eavesdropper is the hansom driver. And that would

4

be quite impossible of the *clip-clop* of hooves and the *rattle* wagon's wheels over cobblestones.

"We have discussed this. Have you the coin?"

I was unable to stash any significant coin while traveling. My father knew every stitch of clothing, every perfume, every minute of my every day.

Sarah, however…was unmonitored. And it was a testament to my level of trust that I had no fear she would flee with the money. She was, for all intents and purposes, my sister. The only company I had ever known, save my mother.

"I 'ave it." Sarah's accent seemed to ring through the carriage.

"Sarah, darling, we must listen to the locals. Try to mimic their accent." I clear my throat. "It shall be a protection," I say, in the best southern drawl I can manage.

"Oo, that is most excellent." She blinks, "I mean, capital."

I wince at her attempt—but it shall have to do.

"Did you secure lodging under the name I provided?"

"Yes, but…" the first quiver of her lips.

"Yes?" I try, try to keep the shake from my hands.

"It shan't last long. Your brother found the money."

"What! When?"

Horror blackens my sight. My brother was cruel, horrid, but oh so clever. He would instantly comprehend why Sarah was carrying a sizeable sum.

She places her hand over mine, "I split it in two. He did not get it all. But…"

5

It would last but a few days.

I stare around the carriage, out at the massive oak trees, flying past the window. We would have to secure a position. Without letters, it may be futile. My mind conjures desperate images. I am not ignorant to the fate of women without protection. Without coin.

"I shall forge them."

Two weeks later

Hunger is a curious thing.

It gradually makes its presence known; first like a tiny little rat, gnawing at one's insides…but soon shifts to a roaring, biting lion, consuming each and every thought.

Three days without a meal. We had taken to…stealing. Wandering into fields at night, gathering bits of vegetables, and eating them on the run.

One would not image one such as I, from a sprawling estate, and a titled father, would have such intimate knowledge.

Hunger and I met on several occasions. Locked in my opulent apartment, for two days' time, with only water, "To clear my head. Make me rethink my position."

When my opinions conflict with fathers. Which would be every solitary word issuing forth from his cruel mouth.

Streaks of red cross the horizon as dawn arrives. The day is beautiful.

Azure sky, with white puffs of clouds, as numerous as the bobbing cotton in the fields on either side of us.

Sarah strides forward, her long legs handling the road better than my own.

I finger the forged papers of recommendation in my skirt.

I see the sign and swallow.

CHARLESTON'S FANCY

The park is remote, but I see in the distance, festive red and white tents, billowing in the salty air.

"Allegra. Look!" Sarah's long finger juts upward.

No less than three hot-air balloons take to the sky and a smile breaks loose. The first in a month.

I squeeze her hand and nod, not trusting my voice. She risked her life for me. I am responsible for us, live or die.

I hear it and my heart beats frantic and discordant—in direct contradiction to the perfect, synchronous notes that spurred the reaction.

An orchestra. I close my eyes and halt, right outside the wrought iron gate, allowing the music to bathe me, fill in the cracks of my soul.

Home. The music is home.

"No. No, no, no. How many times must I tell you?" A very large-walrus-looking man, taps his stick upon the podium at the front of the orchestra.

"Hurry." I grab Sarah's sleeve and we plunge forward, weaving past a throng of people.

From hired hands who screw, tighten and pound, to prim and polished maids, draped with pristine white aprons, carrying trays of sweets that make my stomach scream with hunger. All bustling around a sprawling, white confection of an Inn.

"Take ten." The maestro gives the word and I see the musician's faces alter—some amused, some irritated. All scatter to enjoy each moment of their break.

"Excuse me, good sir."

Walrus-man wheels about, much like a ship changing course, to regard Sarah and I. I swallow as I watch his eyes rove over our definitely-not-pristine attire.

"I am Allegra Teagarden and this is my cousin, Sarah. We are newly arrived and seeking a position. I am a violinist—I—"

"Hold your introduction Miss Teagarden. I am not in need of a violinist."

My insides clench and I fight the swoon. This is our very last chance.

I thrust the papers at him. "I have papers."

He begins to wave them away.

"Hold on, Mr. Plimpton." A deep, baritone voice rumbles behind us.

I turn and a very tall, very dark man ambles forth. Plimpton's bulk somehow deflates smaller and smaller as he draws closer.

"Sir." He nods.

The man extends a long fingered hand. "Silas. I am the owner of this establishment. You say you are a musician."

8

He has not the southern drawl of Charleston. It is decidedly Yankee-northern.

My cheeks are flushed hot-red. His eyes rove over me, and something about the set of his mouth. As if he would devour me whole, if I should allow it.

"Yes, sir. Here are my papers." I thrust them into his hand and he touches it a breath too long. "I…studied with Heir Schubert for a time."

The man's black eyebrows shoot beneath the matching color hair. "Heir Schubert, you say. Plimpton, your impulsivity might have cost us a real find, today."

Plimpton scowls, regarding my clothing with suspicion.

"Might you give us a sample, Miss…" he unfurls the papers, eyes roving, "Teagarden?"

He gestures to the small stage. I stride forward, willing, willing my legs to hold out.

Sarah collapses in a front row seat, primly folding her hands in her lap. She keeps her eyes cast low, probably also trying to remain upright.

He places the violin in my hands. As I slip it beneath my chin, joy ricochets through my soul. And I begin.

The music flows forth from my soul, as I channel emotion, as I was instructed.

Without permission, I begin to hum a melody in counterpoint—so that my music and voice hum together in a polyphony. My perfect pitch ringing throughout the tented amphitheater.

I halt. I have lost track of all time and space, as is my custom when I play.

The seats come back into focus and I see not just

Sarah, but the entire orchestra, hired hands gathered behind them, and small children before me, cross-legged on the ground.

Silas begins a slow, metered clapping, which erupts into thunderous applause and whistles.

Sarah meets my eyes and we share a communal, non-verbal sigh.

"You are hired, Miss Teagarden."

CHAPTER ONE

1860 Charleston, South Carolina
9 months later

I see him, dead-center in the crowd.

My heart seizes then surges against my ribcage, pumping a thick terror all the way to my fingertips. They tingle as I grip the neck of my cello, hastening it between my legs.

The man's form amplifies as if he is the melody and the rest of the people milling past him, the harmony. His soldier's uniform, emblazoned with my father's crest is unmistakable, even at night. Come to find me. To haul me home.

Jonesy notices. As he adjusts his violin beneath his chin, his dark eyes search the crowd for the source of my panic.

"What is it, Allegra?"

I glance around the orchestra, reassuring myself that no other musician's take notice. My fellow cellists are oblivious, smiling and murmuring, awaiting the conductor's call to attention.

"By the boathouse." My voice sounds small and weak. I thrust back my shoulders against it.

Jonesy's eyes flick through the crowd and halt. He nods. "Steady, my friend. We'll shove off in moments."

The riverboat teems with well-heeled Charleston society. Women in ball gowns uselessly flutter fans against the brutal, oppressive heat; even though dusk has fallen, every inhalation is like breathing underwater.

I never thought I'd miss England's rain, but the summer blaze is intolerable.

The last few patrons' board and the boat rumbles as it shudders away from the dock.

Away from the amusement park, away from my wretched hunter.

My relieved breath escapes as my chest struggles to find its normal rhythm.

My eyes flit across the shoreline—the white guesthouse, the white swans and peacocks, and the hovering red and white striped balloon, stark against the darkening night sky.

The amusement park, *Charleston's Fancy,* is both my savior and my master.

The hairs on the back of my neck rise despite the close heat.

Someone else watches. Silas, the grand owner, glares from the dock. His eyes firmly fixed on me, despite the throng covering the deck.

The man misses nothing.

"You're fine now, Allegra. Breathe my friend," Jonesy prompts. His eyes follow my gaze to

Silas. "Forget him. Choke on his importance, he will."

I force a weak smile. "One must have a dream…"

Bang!

I duck. As does half the string section; my heart hammers like the kettledrum behind me as I struggle to catch my breath.

A flaming blue cluster of light cuts across the inky-black sky, hovering for but a blink above the boat. It blossoms into a fiery flower, raining back down to earth as a sparkling waterfall.

Jonesy smiles widely, the sky casting a blue glow across his features. "The pyrotechnics. I forgot they were trying that tonight."

"By their reaction, so did everyone else."

I search the crowd once again, but my seeker is gone. My eyes drift up, searching for the origin of the organized chaos that lights the sky.

On the hill, a man scrambles to and fro, setting the fireworks alight. Four red jets streak heavenward, illuminating his upturned face for a short moment.

I suck in my breath. He is beautiful; tangles of black curls and a long, straight nose and lips. His complexion is dark, exotic.

"Who." I swallow. "Who is that?"

"That be the warlock," Marietta interrupts. She leans forward conspiratorially, so close I am able to make out the light sheen of sweat on her ample bosom as it threatens escape from her scalloped décolletage.

"Everyone's talking about him. His name is LeFroy. He's even newer than you, deary."

"Why do you say he's a witch?"

"Marietta, do not be so provincial. He's not a witch—" Jonesy begins.

"I have it on good authority he *flies*."

"What?" A warm tickle of fear flits across my chest.

The conductor taps his rod and the myriad of instruments rise to his call.

I reposition the cello between my legs and risk one final glance.

The hillside is bare, but the pyrotechnics continue to fly, burst and twinkle as if millions of fireflies dance a frenzied tango.

He is gone.

Brighton

"Jonesy! For heaven's sake man, hurry up!"

Dark clouds cluster, pregnant and oppressive over the bay.

"Keep your shirt on, Captain Bly." Jonesy arrives, whipping supplies and water pell-mell into the dingy.

Crack!

Thunder booms, so close the vibration hums to my core. The sound doesn't bother; indeed, bangs and fizzles are now my life.

I stare heavenward, squinting into the gloom and nod. "Good. Good. We have to hurry, Jones."

Lightning flashes in the bay, *connecting* with the

14

water. White tendrils spread like a glittery film from the core of the strike. Again and again and again, the heavens alight.

One, two, three, four. Not enough strikes.

Swirling clouds twist and turn—rumbling inside, as if some great, dark beast longs for escape.

A few hard drops of rain tap my head, and in a blink, the deluge erupts, dowsing us.

Jonesy's eyes squint against the driving, vertical rain. I clap him hard on the shoulder. "You don't have to do this."

His black eyes steal to the isle in the middle of the bay then flick back to me. "I'm afraid I do. You're daft, LeFroy. So daft, you may drown or fry, depending on your particular death wish."

"Too true," I laugh. "Thank you, my friend."

"Hold up!" A deep booming voice cuts a channel through the fog.

Silas arrives, striding down the launch; his white cane glowing in the gloom. "I need a word, Mr. LeFroy."

"Blast." I clamber out of the boat to face him. "Go on."

The howling wind whips his black hair but those pale, expressionless eyes remain utterly singular. "The receipts were thrice fold tonight because of your little pyrotechnic show. I wish to keep you on indefinitely."

"Indefinitely is a long time."

"Don't be coy, LeFroy. We both know a stroke of my pen could send you running or into shackles."

My hands clench as I will them still, and not around his windpipe. I nod and grimace. "I must go. We will discuss it later."

15

His eyes stray into the bay and back to the dingy. "You truly are mad."

"Yes, yes." I wave, already walking away.

Shoving the boat into the water, I steer it toward *Fire Island* without looking back.

Driving sheets of rain lambast our faces. Jagged bolts of light assault the ground ahead amidst a continuous eruption of white light. It flickers on and off as if God's candle gutters.

Crack after *crack* cut the night as a litany of bolts strike the ground, steaming and sizzling against the rocky crag in the bay. No doubt some of Fancy's newer workers will think it a miracle, of so many bolts in one place. But that is precisely the reason I chose it.

One, two, three, four, five, six...

My heartbeat increases. My magic number; enough voltage.

"So it begins."

The tiny boat skims the choppy waves, rising to catch air and splashing down, slopping seawater over the sides.

Pops and booms of light and sound pock the air above as if a celestial warzone congregates directly overtop the isle.

Jonesy leaps out with furtive glances at the sky. I follow, scrambling into the shallows, to help him secure the boat to the makeshift-dock.

Two cats mewl, winding their way in and out of trees, darting out and back to best avoid the downpour. They finally skitter toward me, embracing their soggy fate.

Jonesy's eyes narrow to stare. "They're waiting. *Outside for you.*" Jonesy shivers, pointing at their soaked faces. "That is blasted unnatural; cats detest water."

I kept my eyes straightforward on the forest to discourage this line of conversation.

"Are you sure you won't need my assistance?" He prompts.

I shake my head, finally meeting his dark gaze. "No. You know too much already. If you weren't so observant *and* obstinate, you could still be blissfully oblivious."

He smiles. "Where's the fun in that?"

The cats mewl louder, edging ever closer.

I ignore them and pelt down the overgrown path toward the briny pond.

"Good luck, Brighton," Jones calls to my back.

I raise my hand in reply without turning and run faster.

CHAPTER TWO

"At least permit me to hot iron your hair," Sarah says, her blue eyes pleading.

"What is the point in that? With this heat, your hard work will melt the moment I step outside. Might you fetch the wig? We're going to be late."

I stare in the looking glass and run my fingers through my hair. For a second, I feel the ghost of my mother's touch, combing out the waves, soothing. "Your strawberry field," she used to call my tangled mess of curls. I swallow down the lump the thought of her brings to my throat.

My eyes flick outside to the Magnolia trees—which remind me of her. *Everything* about this place reminds me of her. It is both painful and comforting.

Her final resting place is here, in Charleston. On our previous tour, she died. Took her own life.

I swallow hard at the memory of returning to England without her. The long, wordless journey home with my father—culminating in the return to our large, lonely estate; where the two of us floated

18

about like two ghosts, steadfastly avoiding contact with one another.

"Here, milady." Sarah hands me a dark brown wig and proceeds to arrange my hair beneath it. She upsweeps the sides to fasten them in place with a Magnolia pin, a gift from my mother. I finger it lovingly.

"How about this one, milady?"

I turn to stare and shake away the trance.

Sarah lays my best dress on the bed, smoothing it gently.

I sigh. Old habits die hard.

I walk over and place my hands bracingly on her shoulders.

"I'm not *milady*. And you no longer have to dress me. I now only own five dresses, and *that* is my best one. We must think differently to survive here, Sarah."

She nods, blue eyes swimming in tears. "I'm sorry, m—Allegra. It's all taking some getting used to."

I bite my lip as the pang of guilt shoots through my chest. "I shouldn't have let you come with me. You should've returned home, Sarah."

Sarah had caught me, mid-flight and insisted on accompanying me.

She shakes her red head furiously, simultaneously whipping the shirtwaist from the armoire. "Don't you ever say that Allegra Manners. I belong *where you are*. I'm not just your lady's maid. I'm your—"

"My friend. I know. My very best friend. And I'm glad you're here, but it still doesn't feel fair. You didn't wish to escape. And remember, it's *Teagarden*."

Her hands fly to cover her blush. "Oh my word, I will give us away yet. You...had much to flee from milady."

A storm crosses her face. I know its origin.

Our eyes search one another's as if sharing the same memory.

My father, veins bulging in his forehead, jabbing his finger against my chest, screaming, "You will marry who I say and you shall do so submissively. If I say roll in the mud, you shall obey. If I say burn that blasted cello—you. Shall. *Obey!*"

I shiver and stare at the sparse surroundings of our bungalow, comparing it to our sprawling estate in the English countryside.

Two beds, a table and chairs, and a threadbare rug before a tiny hearth. I care not. It is all mine and I've earned it—with my own hands, by my music. My index digit smarts as if in agreement. It has been perpetually and troublingly sore for a fortnight.

The music, according to my father, was my most precious commodity. Well, that and my chastity. I was but three when I could first play...and he wasted no time dragging me across the whole of Europe, exploiting me in each and every ballroom across the land.

I shake my head. The future of an entire estate, riding on the slim shoulders of a gangly seven-year-old.

My hands shake and Sarah grasps them hard, squeezing my fingers.

We sink onto the bed's edge, both our chest's heaving. "I...just needed to be more than something to wed. Or somebody's little music box. I...can think. Better than many men."

Sarah nods furiously. "I understand. You were drowning, milady."

The sides of my mouth twitch and curl up a fraction. "Yes, I was. I could not marry him."

Sarah's eyebrows pull together, and I know by the repulsed curling of her lip she recalls my would-be fiancé.

Fat, rich, and cruel Lord Lumberton. Thrice my age and desperate to produce an heir.

My father had no care where I landed, so long as my alliance brought more coin or more prestige to the House of Manners.

My finger, which had long given me trouble from hours of playing, had been the turning point for my father.

He decided my dowry would out-pay what he feared might be the end of my musical career.

My index finger was currently bent, the tip touching my palm. No matter how I tried, I could not straighten it, unless I flicked it up with my other hand.

I did so, and Sarah flinched.

Any semblance of kindness that had lived in Estate Manners had died with my mother. Whose loveless marriage had been arranged. As mine was to be.

I shake my head, needing to explain. "I couldn't have him marry me off. And share mother's fate. At the end…she was so despondent."

"Worried for you, Allegra. And you alone. Not even about herself. Down to the end."

I frown, an edge of anger stealing into my voice, "In the end, she did think of herself."

Sarah shakes her head. "I still do not believe that, Milady."

Thomas, my elder brother, took after my father.

Cruel and handsome and ruthless. Leaving mother and I to try and carve out our own slice of happiness amidst their endless demands of propriety.

My mother died on a visit to Charleston; and even after two years, the place refused to vacate my mind.

So, whilst on our next musical tour of these United States, I fled; escaped his societal halter.

On our last penny, we saw the sign tacked on the pub, as if Providence had seen our plight.

'New Orchestra forming. Musicians apply at Charleston's Fancy.'

"It's an adventure here, Allegra. This...Charleston. New ideas, new opportunities. Why, I may no longer be in service."

I smile wider. "No. We shall find you employment of your choosing. One that pleases you."

"Pleases *me...*" she murmurs in awe.

A harsh rap on the bungalow door startles us both to standing.

I open it to see Silas. He grants me a smile which does not reach his eyes. That smile is familiar; it's merely plastered on a new face.

"A word, Miss Teagarden."

I step outside, shutting the door on Sarah's pinched face.

The amusement park has wakened; ladies and gentlemen in a sparkling array of colors shuffle in two directions, as if they were its colorful arms, stretching before the morning chaos.

Hands erect white tents in preparation for

tonight's society ball. I spy a throng of workers buzzing over the outside of the massive guest house, stringing garlands of flowers like busy human bees.

It is breathtaking. A white, blossoming heaven on earth.

The rich flock to dance, dine, socialize and drink in all the amusements *Charleston's Fancy* offered.

The smell of gardenia, magnolia and honeysuckle waft down into the main thoroughfare where we mere mortals, reside.

I blink, refocusing on Silas's impatient face.

I clear my throat. "Yes, Mr. Boone?"

"The orchestra practices at one sharp." He boldly fingers one of my ringlets, placing it behind my shoulder.

I shiver, fighting the hitch in my chest.

Do not bolt. Steady. He is your vile ticket to freedom.

A young girl skips down the thoroughfare, barely keeping her eyes in their sockets. Her gaze oo'd and aww'd without a whispered sound at the park's untold delights.

Her nanny shoo's her forward, lugging her cello.

Silas raises an eyebrow. "One of yours, I suppose?"

I beam. I cannot help it. "Yes, lessons, you know. I'll be sure to be done by one. Sharp."

He nods. "Good. You have quite an ear, Allegra, and I've heard a rumor you compose as well."

A hot blush warms my cheeks. "Yes."

"Bring one to me."

"I shall, Mr. Boone, thank you."

"Silas. Do call me Silas."

Silas turns and walks toward the main house without another word. His white walking stick swinging jauntily at his side.

I bend and pat the top of Esmeralda's head. "Ready, my dove?"

Behind me, murmurs rise to fevered whispers. I glance back and my heart plummets to my knees, turning them to water.

My eyes meet Sarah's and I give her a nod. She shuffles forward, motioning for them to enter.

"Come in, Essie and Miss Parker. How's your practicing?"

I quietly shut the door and stare, mesmerized. It is the beautiful man from the hillside. The fireworks genius...the dark-haired witch?

He stands before Silas, gesturing wildly, his face taut with rage.

His blue eyes pinch and he spits, "It is far too dangerous. You are begging for trouble. You cannot light it all."

Silas stands straighter. He is slightly taller than the man, but his head cocks as if he is unsure.

I bite my lip. Prior to this moment, *unsure* is the least likely word I would ever pair with Silas Boone. But this man...challenges him.

Indeed, Silas is the second most arrogant man I've ever encountered.

"*You* manage to find a way. Out there, in the middle of nowhere. How is that possible, LeFroy?"

Lefroy. I turn it over in my mouth, permitting the sound of it to linger on my tongue.

LeFroy presses his lips together. "I have explained that, as best I can. I cannot abide by your use of the arc lamps."

"I have never seen them, anywhere. And I being the first to possess them, will be an instant draw to the well-heeled. They are always panting after the latest invention."

LeFroy's eyes narrow, "There is a reason you have never seen them prior.. I tell you, complications will ensue from their use."

"I care not for the complications, only the coin this will bring. Work your magic. I want this place glowing with light. Can't have the rich breaking their necks, can we?"

Chills spread over my neck. Silas…is dangerous. My instincts crawl, urging me to flee.

But what choice do I have?

None.

Mr. LeFroy inhales deep breaths, biting his lip as Silas stalks away.

His eyes suddenly flick to me as if feeling my stare.

I freeze; caught eavesdropping. "H-hello." I raise my hand in a feeble, awkward greeting.

He inclines his head, ever so slightly and turns, stomping in Silas's footsteps toward the guest house. His deep brown hair blows in the morning air as he breaks into a canter.

My heart beats against my chest, well into the next hour, and throughout Essie's scales, recalling every mannerism on his face.

Witch or no, Mr. LeFroy has wholly enchanted me.

Chapter Three

The heat is unrelenting, but a cool breeze blows in from the sea, billowing the white tent like a fore gleam of fall. I sit in my orchestra chair, my cello propped between my thighs, staring out across the white-tipped waves.

A sigh slips from my lips. *I could stay here forever. I intend to.*

I hear the young boy coming before I actually see him. His left club-foot drags behind him, making a loud scraping sound on the hardwood orchestra floor.

Eyes, blue and bright as the heavens, meet mine. "Good day, Ms. Teagarden. I-I was wondering…" The boy is about ten, and his eyes drop to regard his nervously-shuffling feet.

"Yes?"

His earnest eyes rise and plead. "I wish to learn to play. I. I haven't the money for lessons, though. Might I work in exchange, to learn?"

The boy's shirt is far too large; his scuffed boots have passed the day for mending and now beg replacement. I wish for my father's fortune, to help him. I swallow, clearing the lump in my throat.

"Of course. I must first consider your assignment. Come back in a few days' time?"

The boy beams and I see hope spark in his eyes. "Thank you so much, Miss Teagarden. They were right. You really are an angel."

My cheeks heat and feel a stare burning the side of my face; like I am the insect and Lefroy's gaze the magnifying glass.

Mr. LeFroy is checking the newly erected arc lamps. He strides across the lawn and my heart leaps.

A very large hot air balloon darts playfully overhead; its festive red and white stripes like a massive, floating lollipop in the sky. I have never seen one so close and my heart beats like a little girl at the fair for the first time.

I forget myself and my manners and dash after Mr. LeFroy, skidding to a stop by his side.

His thick hands yank the rope and check the tether. He jerks, apparently just registering my presence.

"Where on earth did it come from? How do you keep it aloft?"

Suddenly LeFroy's eyes narrow and see nothing but me. They smolder and burn, hotter than the Carolina sun.

"Are you always so curious, Miss…?"

"Teagarden. Yes. How else does one learn?'

He hesitates; raising one dark eyebrow, then gives a reluctant smile. "Indeed."

My heart stutters like the words that are now stuck between my mind and mouth.

His gaze lingers…curiously flicking from my eyes to my hair and back.

I pat my head. "Something amiss?"

"No, mam."

He starts to walk away, toward the gazebo. "These lamps? I've never seen them before? Where on earth did you get them?"

"Where on earth indeed," he mutters, still walking away.

I suddenly do not wish him to leave. I fight convention's reins, straining against my neck, and force myself not to follow him.

"You did not tell me how it keeps aloft," I blurt, too loud and much too forward.

He turns to face me, still walking backwards. "Curious interests for a female. But if you must know it is a mixture of dilute sulfuric acid and metal fillings. It creates Hydrogen."

I cock my head, trying to make sense of it.

He laughs at my expression and turns again to go, walking briskly. An irrational panic grips my chest and I once again blurt—"What was Silas on about? Where and *how* does one make light from nothing?" Like a schoolgirl, unable to halter her tongue.

LeFroy whirls, his tanned face draining of color; anger screwing up his mouth. I have apparently finally exhausted his patience.

He stalks back and leans in to whisper in my ear, "Miss Teagarden. Are you familiar with the phrase, *curiosity killed the cat?*"

Anger suffuses my face, deepening my blush. But my eyes meet his without a blink. "Have *you* ever heard, curiosity is lying in wait for every secret?"

LeFroy's face changes instantly: his mouth trembles, like a dam holding back his amusement. I hold my breath, unsure.

Suddenly he throws his head back as a deep throaty chuckle spills forth. Gooseflesh erupts from my chest to my toes with the strange, musical sound of it—a forte of breath and laughter. A strange burning sensation erupts on my chest.

He shakes his head slowly, biting the side of his mouth, his eyes intensely regarding me.

"Ralph Waldo Emerson."

My eyebrows rise. "I confess myself shocked. You are a scholar, Mr. LeFroy? A chemist *and* a poet."

"Hardly." He gestures to his work clothes. "Don't judge the man by his fashion." He smirks. "Or lack thereof."

"Squabbling, children?" Jonesy arrives, his violin case in hand, and to my surprise, Sarah bustles close behind. She stands next to him, a whole head taller.

They both seem entirely too pleased for the prospects of such a gruelingly hot work-day.

"I see you've already met Mr. LeFroy," Jonesy prompts as I am apparently struck dumb.

I shake my head. "Not formally. Unless you consider his chastisements an introduction."

LeFroy laughs again and gives a tiny bow, which looks ridiculous against his dirty work clothes. "Pardon my rudeness."

"Miss Allegra Teagarden, may I present Mr. Brighton LeFroy."

A barking scoff from the brass section bade us all turn. Marietta has arrived in a poofed-pink-gown, which looks every bit as bulky and uncomfortable as she does. "Stay away from him, Allegra. I told you, he's a witch."

LeFroy's eyes narrow and harden to blue ice and he tips his hat. "Good day, Ms. Teagarden. I have loads of work and toil before I might return to churning my brew." His eyebrows raise and waggle at Marietta.

"Joke all you like, Mr. LeFroy. I know you work the devil's magic on that blasted isle," Marietta calls to his retreating form.

"Bubble, bubble, toil and trouble," he mutters, his words getting lost in the wind.

My eyes leap between the back of his head and the isle in the bay.

A small, desolate island rambles out of the water like a rocky fortress. Thick overgrown trees make it impossible to see past the shoreline.

He lives there? Alone?

My scalp tingles with an ominous prickle. *Why is a man so obviously educated, here? Working for that beast of a man?*

"Why, indeed. Why are you?" I murmur quietly. Secrets. He has secrets.

Musicians now pour into the tent, taking their respective places in the rows.

Silas parts the fluttering tent door, his eyes evaluating the situation in one fell sweep. They focus and narrow on Jonesy, still not in his seat.

"Percival Jones, I believe you are almost late."

Jonesy's dark eyes flash with anger, but he crams his lips together. He is a prisoner to the park as well. To Silas.

"Coming." He takes his seat beside me in the orchestra row.

Sarah is already departing, her long-legged pace almost comical as she tries in vain to appear nonchalant.

Silas takes his place by Mr. Plimpton, the conductor—who is now self-consciously rubbing his hands over his substantial middle.

Silas possesses a talent for making people recall their flaws, which he then molds, shapes and displays for his own personal use—like some detestable potter of imperfection.

Silas raises his hands and the musicians immediately quiet.

"The riverboat cruise was a tremendous success. Thanks in large part to your accomplished execution of the music, and our new fireworks display. I've already received a flood of new reservations, and the guest house is booked through fall." His eyebrows pull together in disdain. "The rich must have their amusements. And good thing, as it keeps us all in gold. In these tense times-people are hungry for distraction. I want suggestions on how to keep the music fresh? I'm feeling the symphonies going stale."

Mr. Plimpton's cheek twitches, but he holds his tongue. The man is a most excellent conductor, a *maestro*, and Silas is tone-deaf.

Jonesy murmurs, "He always knows best. Whatever the subject, he's an expert."

Silas turns sharply. Tone deaf, but with apparently sharp ears.

He barks, "Mr. Percival Jones. Might you have a

suggestion on how to better the show? Perhaps adding *stilts* for all musicians to wear?"

A few idiots chuckle and I shoot them a death look.

Jonesy doesn't flinch. He is a small man, but darkly handsome. He glares back at Silas with an unwavering gaze.

Silas resumes his droning and I feel Jonesy relax. But his arm, touching mine, still quivers with rage.

Jonesy suddenly interrupts, "Perhaps it's merely time to change the music. Mr. Plimpton is excellent, but our instruments itch to play something new."

Plimpton smiles in gratitude and nods his ascension.

Silas's glare tunnels onto the pair of us and all else falls away.

"Thank you for that fawning review, *Mr. Jones.* We shall consider it. Perhaps *I* will choose the music."

Not a word is spoken, but every chair in the orchestra shifts as the apprehension rolls back the rows in a collective wave as buoyant as the nearby surf.

A flash of color in the distance quickens my heart. My eyes flick, searching for the familiar red crest of the uniform, but it is merely LeFroy's striped balloon, waving in the sea breeze.

I swallow, trying to regain composure.

I think of the soldier, sent from father. *So close...too close.*

I scratch under my wig, fidgeting.

Jonesy smirks and tips his head, indicating my tilted hair.

I readjust it and sigh. I doubt my disguise will conceal me much longer. My fingers stray to my singular earring, which I'd mounted as a pendant around my neck.

I lovingly trace the magnolia, a gift from my mother.

My nanny related she'd scoured the countryside for a silversmith capable of such a delicate hand.

I'd worn the set every solitary day since she passed. Since she left me.

My eyes fill. Only one earring remains. I'd lost the other in my mad-dash escape from father.

"A masquerade!" I blurt.

Every musician in front and behind turns to stare as my face threatens to burn to ash.

Silas stares. The orchestra holds its breath.

He smiles and the relief about me is palpable. I almost hear muscles relaxing.

"Yes. That is a *most excellent* suggestion, Miss Allegra. A masquerade. For musicians and guests alike. I like it."

He stalks off, waving his hand, calling over his shoulder. "Carry on, Plimpton."

Excited murmurs course through the crowd as Plimpton taps his podium for order.

Jonesy leans over. "The world might be ending."

"What?"

"Silas uttered a compliment. You best be careful, deary. I believe that dragon fancies you."

I shudder, thinking of the wildness of Silas's eyes, hoping Jonesy is wrong.

But he rarely is.

A fortnight later

My stomach knots beneath my hand as I wander along the rocky shore. The sun is saying its good-byes, disappearing in a final reddish-golden slip below the horizon as the crying gulls overhead seem to lament its return to bed.

"This is madness."

The hem of my dress skims the top of the white-frothy shallows and I gather it with both hands, carelessly exposing my ankles.

"Where are you, Brighton?" I murmur quietly.

A spout of water explodes heavenward from the surf, raining down in a million tiny circles. A dolphin rises to the surface, expelling air from her blowhole. She clicks and another slices through the water beside her.

I sigh. Mr. LeFroy has been conspicuously absent. As if our teasing conversation had prompted him to avoid me.

Over the past weeks I've only seen him twice. Each time he was enroute across the bay to the jagged isle he apparently calls home.

I've taken to stalking this moonlit shore, staring at it from across the ever-choppy waves.

Something about the isle is amiss.

My stomach tightens as a flash of heat -lightning paints the sky.

The air seems to *shrink*, growing close and dense, as if I am *breathing in* the warm shallows at my feet.

The warming on my chest returns and I scratch it.

The dolphin's issue a final chastising click and plunge beneath the waves, leaving me alone. As if they know *something* approaches.

As if they are far smarter than I, quickly plunging to the safety of the depths.

I hold my breath as my eyes transfix upon the stony isle.

Thunder rumbles.

The island *shimmers.*

Like the heat at high noon.

I blink, pressing the heel of my palms to my eyes, shaking my head.

They pop open wide and I long for a spyglass. I vow to buy one.

Heat wafts from the isle in wavering fits and starts. It *blurs* and *solidifies. Blurs* and *solidifies,* before my eyes.

I hear my gasp as if from another's mouth.

I pace, splashing back and forth through the shallows; the water lapping up, over, and into my boots. My eyes transfixed upon the craggy rock.

There is more to come. I know it. Every night I come.

And every night I question my sanity. Almost a one-way ticket to Bedlam.

The island grows brighter and I freeze, and drop to the shallows, vaguely registering the pull of the waves against my knees. A warm tingle begins upon my chest.

Lights. Tiny, twinkling, myriads of lights, move in clusters like tiny fairies across the rocky isle's shore.

My hand shoots to cover my mouth. Their

movements are erratic. They are most definitely alive. But what, what could they be? *Fairies?*

I snort aloud. *I don't believe in make-believe creatures.*

"Fireflies?" My lips twist angrily. "This is madness. I must know."

The creatures flit in a congregation toward a tree and spiral down its trunk in a helix of white light, which blinks on and off at varying intervals. Like some ethereal natural lighthouse.

Something in the patterns of the light jar loose a memory. My father's finger, tap-tap-tapping.

The blood in my veins goes cold as the rain, just beginning to fall.

"Is that. Is that Morse code?"

I falter upright and as if struck headlong and drop my dress back into the surf. A gull screams and scolds directly overhead as Goosebumps explode across my chest.

Cats.

A herd of them. Too close to the shore to be natural.

Their calls rise every second, carrying across the bay like a mewling nursery of newborn babes.

"Oh. My. Word." I am rooted, awash in the surf, as the growing tap-tap-tap of rain on the top of my head increases.

The lights dart from the tree and hover directly over the cats.

One large Tom stops his caterwauling and playfully bats at the circling light. The light dips and splutters, flying crazily as if stunned.

The lights dance into a circle, and descend upon the two large felines in the center. They…

I slump back into the surf; the water sloshing over my thighs.

The creatures wrap about their necks like a collar borne of light.

My heart catapults, beating my ribs to a pulp.

I shake my head in disbelief. "This is unnatural. So unnatural."

Out in the bay, another eruption of mist from a very large blowhole. A whale is hovering about the isle, meandering in the bay between it and my shoreline.

Are the animals drawn to him?

The thought of his beautiful blue eyes, which somehow seem both melancholy *and* hopeful, and the playful smile he gifted me when he forgot himself. Forgot to be sad.

"Brighton. What *are* you doing out there?" I whisper.

The urge to know grips my chest, tightening it.

I look left and right, searching for a dingy.

"Allegra?"

I jump at the voice, and spin to see Sarah trudging across the sand dunes toward the shore.

"Oh my stars, what *are* you doing in the water? You're utterly drenched? And it's raining. Have you gone mad?"

Yes.

Sarah's wide eyes meet mine ad she hovers along the waterline. She hesitates; walking forward and retreating back with the tide's rhythm like a skittish heron.

I stand as torrents of water cascade from my hemline. "I. I."

*If Sarah saw...*I feel the distinct need to protect him.

37

The vision of pitchforks and lanterns and hanging invade my mind's eye.

It was no longer Salem, but *this level of oddness* would most surely have inquiries and consequences.

Sarah's eyes steal to the isle and mine follow. I open my mouth, ready to explain away LeFroy's damnation.

But it is dark. No cats. No lights. Nothing but a glowering crag in the water.

Her eyes turn away, satisfied.

"Silas has come with a surprise. Hurry. You are a mess!"

I walk, and drip, toward Sarah, still reeling.

As I follow her up the path through the sand dunes, one repeating thought echoes, *Is he a witch? Am I smitten with a witch?*

CHAPTER FOUR

"Allegra, you must try it on." Sarah's face pinches with awe and concern.

Silas looks like the cat that has eaten an aviary of canaries. "Yes. I spared no expense. For either of you." He is utterly pleased with himself.

I lift the masquerade gown to hold it gingerly against my chest. It *is truly* magnificent. The bodice is an imperial violet, overlaid by black lace, gathered to the hip by a sunburst yellow bow.

I kick out my leg, admiring the damasked colors of alternating black-grape and Tuscan-red about a full white center.

I am no stranger to gifts, and know they always come with a price. Father showered me with presents from my very first touring recital about Europe.

My tiny self, however, soon learned these fancies were as transient as an English sky.

Father was just as likely to cast them into the fire as he was to give them.

Silas thrusts out his hand. "The finishing touch."

The sequined masquerade mask is adorned with matching colored feathers, which grow like wings from the sides.

I nearly clap in delight. Sarah beams back, misreading my joy.

I will be virtually unrecognizable.

"I…haven't the words to thank you."

"Nor I." Sarah clutches her equally fantastic gown of candlelit ivory. Its V waist and scalloped gathers remind one of a cross between a wedding gown and a regal princess. Irony spreads my lips into an eager smile. Sarah could be the titled one.

"Oh, I am sure I shall think of something."

Something in his voice conjures a shiver.

Silas turns to open and step through the door, leaving a gust of night air in his wake which blows the temporary happiness from the room.

Sarah's anxious eyes meet mine and we both dress in silence.

The night is utter perfection. To accent the white flowered house, Silas, ever the showman, arranged for a thick flock of swans to be released into the black waters the moment our riverboat leaves the dock.

Some now skate across the lake, whilst others skitter about as white ghosts along the bay shore.

'Oohs and Ahhs,' lilt behind me in a myriad of ladies voices. The riverboat is brimming with all of Charleston's high society.

Silas stands on the dock, staring at the vessel like a lover. It is his salvation…at least monetarily.

I smooth my new dress and Jonesy gives me an approving nod.

I lean to whisper, "It's perfect. He shall never recognize me now."

Two well-to-do men nod and smile as they pass. One dressed as an obvious dragon, the other an ambiguous…toad?

Jonesy's raises a thick brow. "Really? You might not be recognized as *you*. But that costume, I'm afraid, makes you stand out like a gazelle among goats."

My face burns and my fingers flit nervously about the hem like frantic birds. "You mean the costume will *draw* attention?"

Jonesy laughs. "*You,* my dear, will draw attention no matter how you try to blend in. You're utterly breathtaking."

His eyes skate across my face. "But you really don't know that, do you?"

Sarah swishes to his side. His eyes instantly leave me and see nothing else but her face. His hand strays, clandestine, to her side, to gently smooth her fingertips and I am struck with revelation.

They are in love.

A wave of gratefulness sweeps through my chest. Sarah so deserves to be loved. And by just such a man. Fear and longing pushes the sentiment out, leaving a hollow space in my chest.

I wish to be loved. But not just any love.

For what I've seen, to be alone is better than to be yoked in lovelessness.

"Allegra?" Sarah searches my face. She always knows, can instantly read my distress.

"I am fine. You best get along. The guests will complain without a proper waitress."

She nods to us both and disappears into the ever-thickening crowd of multi-colored masks.

The boat shudders away from the port and Silas leaps dramatically aboard at the last possible moment. His booming voice cutting across the murmuring throng.

"Good evening. We welcome you to Charleston's Fancy, where all things are possible. We have a spectacular show prepared for you, designed to tempt all your senses. And our guest house still has two openings, if, after partaking you are too overwhelmed and inclined to stay."

He nods to the Maestro Plimpton. "Without further ado."

The riverboat pulls away from the mainland and the violin quartet begins their customary introductory interlude.

My eyes sweep the hillside. Something moves in the dark. My heart climbs to my mouth. I struggle to focus on my surroundings, wanting only to see him. It has been a fortnight.

Brighton.

Mr. Plimpton raises his hands and our instruments follow suite as if the whole orchestra are marionettes, attached to his baton.

Crrack!

Ladies and men alike startle in a collective jump. With a few nervous chuckles, all eyes shoot heavenward.

An eruption of red rockets speed toward one another, detonating seconds before impact into white sparkles which linger, glittering in the sky like ethereal diamonds.

I stare, enraptured.

"Allegra," Jonesy whispers.

The music begins. A piece by Bach.

I know it by heart, my fingers need no minding; they trace the path on my strings like a familiar road. I need not read the music. Truth be told, I only need to read the music once.

My eyes flick between the hill and the sky like a metronome as my heartbeat pounds in my ears, my breath heaving my chest. My fingers pluck the piece of their own accord.

Two, four, six starbursts explode; the very colors of my gown.

Brighton sets gaslights blazing, one by one, which flicker and are somehow magnified, perhaps by prisms? An eerie mist rises across the hillside, hiding him from me. I grind my teeth in irritation, a primal need to imbibe of his presence, overwhelming every bit of me.

I stare at Marietta in the row ahead of me and see the gooseflesh on her pudgy arm. She has seen him as well.

He has not departed. Please, let him still be up there.

My chest aches. I fight the urge to cast down the cello and leap into the bay; to swim and swim. Till I find him, wet and cold, and let his skin warm mine.

Constant explosions light the sky, white and cornflower blue, raining down across the bay, again and again like luminescent raindrops.

The light show reflects in the water, mirror-like, like Alice's Wonderland looking glass, come to life.

I picture the upturned faces of mermaids and sea creatures staring up at the surface in awe.

And my fingers *stray.*

The mourning tune they play does not match the joy and rebelliousness of the dancing lights overhead. Of his soul.

I stray from the piece. Throwing the entire orchestra off.

The music halts in a jangle of discordant notes. Except for my cello.

I compose on command.

I stare, enraptured by the lights, my arm sawing in perfect synchrony with every burst of light. I wince in pain as my fingers stroke the neck of my cello, following Brighton's lead.

With every fiery burst of color, *staccato notes.* With streaming showers of sparks—*long, melodic pulls of my bow across the vibrating strings.*

Jonesy recovers first. He accompanies me, following my lead on his violin, as best he can.

A few brave souls follow suite, their instruments playing harmony about my melody.

All the patron's eyes stray back to the sky. Out of the corner of my eye, I see a woman cover her chest, overcome with emotion.

I spy another couple join hands and a third press her trembling lips together at the beauty—the marriage of light and sound.

I writhe and ache, following his lead, keeping time with his lights with my fingers.

His lights tell a story, as does my music.

It is as if our minds are dancing, sharing a wavelength, and he doesn't even know it.

Or does he?

I finally see him, through the mist. His face severe with emotion, his head cocked in question.

The boat is close enough he can hear the music. My music.

His stare skips through the crowd till he finds me and our eyes connect.

Gooseflesh tears across my chest, down my back and stomach. The heat on my chest relights and I fight the urge to scratch it.

Finally the show concludes in a maelstrom of *booms* and *pop, pop, pops* of sparkling blazes. As if heaven has exploded, and its stars are escaping to earth.

I halt, chest heaving, sweating and breathless.

Fear stops my heart, *realizing what I've done.*

Jonesy's foot taps in anxious accord with my heartbeat.

Then a great resounding, *applause*. It rings through the night, almost as loudly as Brighton's fireworks.

Men and women shoot to a standing ovation. It begins on the lower deck, and then spreads like an ocean wave to engulf the upper as well.

My eyes find Silas—his face beet-red. But as he observes the crowd's reaction, his expression gives way to rapture, and he too begins to slowly clap. My stomach plummets to wallow in relief to my boots.

Brighton turns his stare to me, with the same worshipful gaze, for a heart-halting moment.

And is gone.

After my victory on the riverboat, my bed

couldn't hold me. Sleep eluded me much the same way the cool winds tried but could never quite manage to breech the ever-warm Charleston shallows.

I steal out of the cottage, praying Sarah will not wake and panic in my absence.

I know my plan to be foolish. I know, if caught, I will at best, lose employment—my weak tether to freedom—or at worst, lose my life?

If Brighton is dangerous.

The sour taste of fear floods my mouth.

But a hidden *something* in his dark blue eyes made me doubt that gruff façade.

Jonesy would scoff and tie me to a chair for such weak reasoning, but Jonesy is not here.

I approach the dingy and scramble into it with a quick glance over my shoulder.

The water slops over the boat's side, and I begin to fervently row; my thoughts straying to Monsieur Lafayette, my father's security chief. The man was the sole reason I had ever learnt any practical task. Otherwise, I would've been bound to drift through this world, my only knowledge to compose music and attend tea.

I steer the boat with confidence, picturing our many escapes to the Lake Country while father was away on business.

Truth be told, I would not have managed my escape without him.

With knowledge, even simple, everyday knowledge, comes power.

The dingy approaches the isle. I hold my breath, my eyes scouring the shore but this eve, nothing appears out of the ordinary.

The boat makes the crossing to Fire Isle quickly in the calm water of the night.

As if the bloody rock is expecting me.

Ridiculous.

I shiver nonetheless.

This is the name whispered in the parlor's back home. Near Fire Island, Charleston. Where my mother drown. Where she took her life.

Swinging my legs over the side, I slosh into the shallows to secure the boat.

I turn to stare at the shore from whence I came. Snowy egrets and pelicans dot the surf, bobbing up and down like feathery buoys. But here…nothing.

No birds.

I secure the dingy and hurry from the water, light-headed from the steady pounding of my heart.

Tearing my eyes away from the Charleston shore and relative safety, I slink into the foliage. The isle is like a fae place; its green ferns swallow my feet as easily as the moss which gloms to the trunk of every tree. Resurrection fern, they call it. I shiver at the pun.

What am I looking for? This is madness.

I finger the pistol Jonesy thrust upon me.

Once he heard my story, he insisted I needed protection. And had insisted on training me to use it. Which had been no small feat. We'd have to leave Charleston proper for any sort of privacy.

The rush of flowing water calls somewhere to my right. If a dwelling existed on this craggy rock, it would most definitely be near the water. I keep pace alongside it, skulking through the deep green ferns, never letting the undercurrent leave my hearing.

My eyes dart back and forth, searching for alligators. No doubt the isle is crawling with them.

Fire Isle. I knew why the locals called it such. Storms supposedly occurred over the island more than anywhere else in Charleston. But I had not yet seen evidence to warrant that name.

Night birds call as dusk descends in earnest. Fear grips my chest, squeezing my airway shut.

I have a light—but should I use it?

Soon it shall be utterly black and I will be paralyzed, afraid to move through the wood without its reassurance glow to guide my steps.

Fear's metallic taste fills my mouth. The dark. I am not so fearless to be caught here without light.

I can still see where the woods break to the beach. Embracing defeat, I pick my way through newly downed trees toward the moonlight. I bolt and soon stand on the beach, chest heaving, regretting my impulsivity. And equally detesting my cowardice.

I hear them, then.

Cats. A plethora of cats. Mewling and calling back and forth in an off-kilter symphony with the night-birds overhead.

I step out of the safety of the moonlight to follow their other-worldly cries.

I hurry closer and closer, their calls growing louder with each step.

In minutes I arrive. They call and twirl, rubbing their furry bodies against a rambling stone cottage.

Could Brighton live here?

It wasn't squalor precisely, indeed the big beautiful flowers crawling up the bricks painted it quaint, but he seemed too...*grand* for such a small home.

Inhaling deeply, I try to control my frantic heart as I head toward the dwelling.

Hiding in the trees, I wait, but no sign of life, no light erupts at my presence.

Emboldened, I leave the cover of the trees. The cats halt their mewling, staring at my approach.

I freeze. Out in the open, utterly exposed.

One orange striped feline tentatively approaches my leg and sniffs. Its stare meets mine and the world lurches. Its queer yellow eyes looked too deep, somehow, too expressive.

It breaks the contest and pads forward to rub and purr and wind about my leg. I bound toward the window.

I stand on tip-toes to peer through the window.

My breath exhales in relief. *What was I expecting? Cauldrons? Sacrificial animals?*

Reluctantly I admit, "Perhaps."

Two microscopes, ink bottles, parchments and half-eaten plates of food litter a scrubbed wood table. As if Brighton had departed in a hurry.

He obviously had very little, or very poor domestics.

I permit my eye to slide across the open rafters. Odd contraptions hang from the ceiling and are scattered across multiple tables; metal humbugs for which I have no name. Some whirr, some seem to *hum*, but all are unknown.

Emboldened by the silence, I rush to the side door and slide quietly inside.

A metallic pole totters as I open the door and I lunge, catching it before it clatters to the floor. My breath escapes my lips in tiny puffs of flustered panic. One false move will give away my dangerous game of eavesdropping and skulking.

I ease the pole upright, propping it against the wall.

My heart freezes as I register the myriad of glinting silver sparkles interspersed throughout the gloom.

The room is *full* of them—twenty, perhaps thirty, of the silver rods lean against the walls like metallic sentries. I shiver convulsively as I picture them animating and surrounding me, holding me captive till Brighton returns.

A warm tingle begins just below my breastbone. I scratch it. I am ever prone to rashes and itches. Some dangerously so.

"What…are those?"

The breeze creaking through the eaves wakes me from the revelry. My time here is precious.

I fly to the table where two massive, leather-bound volumes lie beside a half-eaten loaf of bread.

The warmth between my breasts intensifies and I flinch. "Ooch."

I touch the leather cover and blink and I cock my head. A tiny jolt ripples through my fingertips at first contact, but so briefly, I doubt its occurrence.

I stare at the volume and whisper the title, ***"Elementi."***

I wrench it open, flipping through pages.

"Tell me everything,"I whisper to it.

My eyes halt, registering a change in the script.

On one page, the usually pristine handwriting denigrates to illegible squiggles.

'I believe I have found the answer. If I may only find the correct amount of current, combined with the correct chemical composition...all things may be possible. And within my reach.'

Gooseflesh explodes down my arms as I shake my head.

Not witchcraft, I do not think. But it does not sound...natural.

I pause, holding perfectly still. *Something* has changed in my environment, but all I hear is my heartbeat in my ears.

Silence. Crickets are quiet. Cats are quiet.

Someone is coming.

I slam the volume shut and bolt toward the window, half-falling, half-scrambling through the frame. My knees scrape the stony ground and I stifle the whimper. I feel the hot rush of blood trickle down my leg and limp over to hunker down in the false comfort of the trees and high ferns.

Light flickers on the cottage and footsteps shuffle inside.

I turn and pick my way through the underbrush toward the beach, not chancing a backward glance.

I press on with my hurried limping; not pausing till my feet strike the bottom of the dingy.

My muscles ache as I franticly row and row, putting distance between me and the words.

"All things may be possible."

CHAPTER FIVE

Silas paces before us, his hands clasped behind his back. "So, I wish you to craft at least three original compositions, choreographed to match Brighton's impressive light show."

My eyes tick between Silas and Brighton. The tension in the air is as brittle and volatile as the driftwood lining the beaches. And I suspect one wrong word from either will ignite and combust the façade of calm within this room.

Silas rubs his hands together so fast I fear they will spark and light the atmosphere ablaze.

"Original scores. Understood?" His black gaze zeroes on Brighton.

LeFroy's body sits rigidly upon the edge of his chair, as if ready to *down* Silas.

I shift uncomfortably and clear my throat. "I *do* love composition, Silas, and I adore what Mr. LeFroy's done with his pyrotechnics—so it shouldn't be so very difficult."

LeFroy shakes his head. Silas seems to comprehend its meaning, but it is lost on me.

"Ah, ah, *ah*, Brighton." He waggles a long finger. "I need not remind you in front of the lady, of your...*responsibilities*, do I?"

LeFroy's teeth grind together. "No. Fine. Miss Teagarden—"

"You may call me Allegra."

The tension in his face lessens a fraction. "Fine. Allegra. I shall meet you this afternoon to begin our assignment. The sooner I might tick it off my growing list of *responsibilities*, the better."

Lefroy shoots to stand and flings open the door. He strides out without bothering to close it.

Silas tsk, tsk's to his retreating back. "Temper, temper."

Silas is not angry, indeed he appears highly amused. He smiles widely at me, but his wide white teeth threaten. "You seem more pleased at the prospect, Allegra."

I nod.

My pleasure has naught to do with composition.

I will get to spend much time in Brighton's company. And despite his tempestuous mood swings, *that* is indeed a most pleasurable prospect.

Brighton

I heard it first and a wave of heat passed over my skin.

My own personal siren call. *Thunder.* My would-be savior and my grim reaper.

Lightning flashes; the sky awakens with bursting white flashes, illuminating the purple backdrop of churning clouds.

I leap out of bed, shaking the cobwebs from my mind.

A bolt strikes close, very very close.

I startle backward and smack my head off the birdcage behind me. Close, too close—six feet from my window the ground hisses and sizzles.

I *feel* his presence before he speaks. A warming sensation, as if I've downed a tumbler of fine scotch, trickles from my spine to my fingers to my toes.

I *stiffen*, awaiting the familiar, sing-song voice.

"Brighton. I am come." His voice from behind the front door.

No use in barricading it. If he wished to enter, he would enter.

I spin, rummaging through my papers on the table, futilely trying to hide the most recent research.

"How? How did you find me again? I was so meticulous," I say, without turning around.

He gives a quiet laugh, his footsteps walking toward me. "You can run, but you can't hide."

Anger scorches my cheeks. I whirl and push past him, loading my arms with the lightning rods.

"If we work together, we might accomplish our goal more quickly."

My hands shake as I fight the urge to strike and pummel that smug look from his haughty-pointed-face. "Our *goals*, couldn't be more diametrically opposed."

He glows, ever-so-slightly, like the warning sky before a storm.

I twist the door knob with my two free fingers, kicking it open with my boot-heel.

"You shall not succeed without me." His voice is scathing as I shove past him.

I push into the storm, running down the path toward the pond in the center of the isle.

The fireflies descend instantly, gathering and trailing behind me as if I am some ethereal Pied Piper. And predictably, the cats arrive as well, falling in step like the soldiers of the cursed that we are.

I sigh. *Innocent bystanders to my madness.*

Water pounds my head, and I thrust on the hat to divert the waterfall occluding my vision.

I sprint around the pond's edge, jamming the lightning rods into the mud till they resemble silver turrets guarding the water.

The pool *flickers*; first with reflection of the maelstrom overhead…but soon the skies quiet and the pool's surface continues to undulate.

A current pops and ripples as an image flits by so quickly, one not ready to see would've missed it.

The evening breeze is like a sigh and I wait, holding my breath.

Lightning *flashes* and I count, "One, two, three—" and thunder cuts across, too quickly, drowning away my voice.

"It's moving away." Disappointment douses my heart. Each and every time I steel myself, prepare my heart and mind, but always that traitor, hope, finds its way about my defenses.

My knees buckle and I crumple before the poles, gritting my teeth against the pain. I place my hands between them, wishing for the thickened, gauzy air necessary for my quest.

"Brighton, you will not succeed without me."

I stare at the pool, not giving him the satisfaction of my expression. "Leave me. Now."

CHAPTER SIX

LeFroy stares out the window, his brow creased in thought. He remains statue-still, as he has for the past quarter hour, oblivious to the late afternoon sun that bathes his face in a beautiful golden-amber.

I stare intently, reveling in the rare opportunity to drink in his features.

His dark curly hair is in need of a cutting and his thin lips turn down as he absently bites the side of his nail, lost to himself. He is not a classic beauty—but the *singularity* of his face demand's attention.

Not all women would swoon for him. But something about him draws me...makes him utterly irresistible.

The warmth on my chest again. Almost *hot* this time. I struggle not to look down my dress to examine what I imagined to be an inevitable rash, but all I see is the Magnolia pattern—the patch on my dress, lovingly sewn by my mother's hand.

I banish the thought. *I shall not think on her now.*

Brighton clears his throat, driving away my mother's ghost and I struggle for words. When he regu. ...ny tongue seems to shrivel in my mouth.

It is his eyes. They...*speak*. Sometimes whisper, sometimes shout.

They now squint, as whatever vexing scenario playing on his mind continues to dominate his demeanor. He doesn't move. Doesn't speak.

I clear *my* throat. "So, Mr. LeFroy, shall we discuss the next pyrotechnics show. Or do you think me a mind reader?" I tease, hoping to smooth out those creases on his brow. He is too very young to have such lines already.

I picture running my fingers across them, kissing them away and shake my head.

His blue eyes finally flick to mine. "Please, call me Brighton. And might I call you Allegra?"

I swallow. *Such intimacy.* "Brighton, then. And yes, you may call me Allegra. The *lights*, sir?"

His lips burst into a smile. "I have some ideas, but they're difficult to put to words. Have you any parchment?"

I nod and walk past him, down the hallway to Sarah's room. I am suddenly aware we are wholly unchaperoned.

No one in Charleston cares a fig for propriety or my chastity. My heart lurches, pumping a tumultuous wave of excitement and worry through my veins.

Reaching her desk, I rifle through the messy collage of Sarah's life.

My fingers touch the paper as I feel him, nay, *smell him* behind me.

Woodsy and enticing. I close my eyes and breathe deeper.

"Thank you. Those will do." He speaks the words gruffly as if filled with emotion and I picture him in bed, surrounded by blankets. And me.

I turn, hoping my blush doesn't bely the thoughts in my mind.

He nods. "Back to the sitting room? It's only proper," he mumbles, eyes dropping to the carpet as if reading my thoughts.

Or having the same.

He strides back out into the hallway without waiting for my answer.

I follow to the sitting room. He is already hunched over the desk, his fingers sketching furiously as I sweep up behind him to stare over his shoulder.

My breath intakes sharply at the life-like sketches.

Pyrotechnics *explode* on the page in a vertical fashion—the first five, starbursts with long comet tails, the next, six diagonal shooting jets, all detonating at once into flower-shaped pinnacles of light.

"Is this better?" His eyes steal up to mine. Again, pouring over my face.

They suddenly drop to the magnolia pendant around my neck.

He spins so his whole body faces me. "What is your story, Allegra?"

Fear tickles my face. "Whatever do you mean, sir?"

He shakes his head. "You were not *born* poor. Your speech, your manners, your walk, your musical education—all recommend you are *high-born*, Miss Teagarden." He smiles. "If that is truly your name." His face clouds again.

I swallow as panic roots in my chest. *What if I was wrong? What if I've misjudged him? He may turn me in for a reward today.* This very moment.

"My parents have passed. I have only distant relatives to recommend me. I and my cousin Sarah, had to find a means to *live*, Mr. LeFroy."

"I said, call me Brighton." His eyes narrow. "Humbug. Sarah is no more your cousin than I am your husband. You are *hiding*...from someone or something. I wish to know before I entangle myself into your world. I have enough to be getting on with as it is."

Anger replaces my fear.

His haughty disposition and lack of empathy light a fire in my chest.

"My *life* is no concern of yours. Need I remind you, you are here to create *a show*. A show to keep this place afloat. That is all. I owe you no explanations. Nor any man, anything."

"Ah." He nods smugly. "You *are* running from a husband."

"What? No!" My hands tremble with rage and I press them hard against my thighs. To keep from striking him.

His gaze ticks from my face, lingering on them. The result is a tremor so violent, it is as if I've been struck with palsy. Except for my one wretched finger. It remains bent, like a crone's hooked claw, its tip firmly fixed against my palm.

He hesitates, but then kneels before me and slides his rough fingers atop mine to gently extricate them from my thigh; the remnant of his touch burns my skin.

His other hand reaches up to finger the magnolia

60

dangling below my collarbone. I flinch as a spark of electricity hits my chest.

He drops it quickly looking alarmed, and points to it instead.

"*This.* This says you were well-loved, my dear. It is very fine. I've upset you. That was not my intent. Do tell me, where is the other earring?"

"How did you know it was an earring?"

He shrugs. "Quite easily. Where is it?"

"Lost." *Like me.*

"You shouldn't wear it—it gives away your game. Anyone with one wit of sense will figure out you're a fugitive with one glance of your fine necklace against your peasant dress."

So stupid. I step forward, feeling dizzy. He steadies me, easing me into a chair. He kneels before me, his chest pressing against my knee. My heart swells, filling my ribcage, pumping madly in my chest.

His proximity sucks every bit of breath from my body. I will myself not to touch him. To reach up and lose myself in the texture of those blackened curls.

"I. I…" I lick my dry lips, trying my best to form coherent words.

"I will not harm you, Allegra. You, and your secrets are safe with me. I have my own…troubles. Too much to ever add to anyone else's. Keep your secrets for now, and keep them close. But if you are ever in need of help, know you may come to me."

I nod. No words come forth. They seem to have been washed away in the pounding river of blood pumping from my ridiculous, smitten heart.

He stands and my breath returns.

He strides to my cello and walks it back, placing it before me. "Play. I will hold the pictures for you to compose."

I place the cello between my legs as he lifts the sketches. He sits directly across from me in a wingback chair and holds aloft the starburst.

I stare at it, my mind bringing it to life, infusing it with color and sound.

I give the bow a tentative pull across the strings. My mind *explodes* with images, travelling down my limbs, expelling out my fingertips.

In a breath, the dance begins; my fingers racing up and down the cello's neck, struggling to keep pace with the sound and images pouring from my head.

The feel of the sturdy wood between my knees emboldens me, its vibration humming through me like a moody lullaby.

We meld. I forget Lefroy; the instrument and I become one.

My feelings—*pain, desolation, desertion, longing*—pour into notes, saturating the room. Brighton disappears. I barely realize when he flips the pages, focusing solely on his sketches.

On the light. On a place where only goodness reigns.

Where I might be happy, and no longer afraid with every step I take.

And much too soon…his hands are empty.

The images halt, breaking my trance.

The silence in the room from the lack of notes leaves a ringing in my ears and I shake my head.

Brighton's eyes are wide and his chest is heaving. A trickle of sweat cuts down the side of his face, past his sideburn. He quickly swipes it with the back of his hand and presses his thin lips together.

His blue-green eyes *blaze*. I shiver, gooseflesh erupting down my neck into my décolletage. He blinks rapidly, breaking our near-enchanted state.

I wrestle to keep the disappointment from my face.

He stands and strides for the door. "I. I must go. That was…" he turns back to stare at me, chest still rising—"*Magnificent.*"

He swallows and bends for his bag. He tosses something toward me, and my shaking hands manage to catch it.

"Whatever is this?"

"Henna." He nods to my head. "Whatever your hair color beneath that wig—your eyebrows do not match. Another give-away. You may color them with that."

My mouth pops open and he slides out before I can manage another word.

Despite our lack of physical contact, I wonder if my own wedding night could ever have more passion.

Evenings later

I should not be here. Stalking the shore, stealing a boat once again. This act alone is scandalous if I am discovered.

Eavesdropping, spying again. If this man wanted

me to know his secrets, he would've told me himself.

The isle is quiet, the ride across the waves suspiciously uneventful.

As if I am supposed to come this night.

But something *draws me* to Brighton.

It is like he is a magneto-stone and my heart and mind are helpless to the attraction.

It vexes me on many levels.

In truth, I've avoided men most of my life. My father, my brother—both difficult and cruel—made me think the entire gender hopeless.

But him. Despite his intensity, despite his gruffness...I sense *more*, when I look at him.

Like these secrets he holds, he longs to tell...someone. The right someone. He is a mystery waiting to be solved.

I feel the yearning—the draw in my chest. My heart all but sings, like a beautiful but demanding siren song.

I am the moth and Fire Island the flame.

I bite my lip. "Yes. And if they get too close, they are incinerated."

The boat arrives in the shadows and I quickly secure it.

I slink my way into the forest from the beachhead, absently picking off the burrs which cling to my skirt from the thick underbrush.

Thunder rumbles overhead, once again threatening. I stand straight up.

The murmur of voices, very close.

This time, not in the direction of the cottage. I see a clearly defined path through the trees and swiftly half-run toward the sounds.

I carefully cut through underbrush till I reach the pond and shift closer into the swampy grass, till I can discern their conversation.

Jonesy and Brighton walk the edge of a very large pond. The bright white moon reflects in its still surface.

"Is this fine for the rod?"

Jonesy stabs another of the silver poles into the mud, his face grimacing with the effort. The very silver sentries who almost gave me away on my last visit.

"You know, we are taught to *hide* from lightning, not will it to us, LeFroy."

Brighton's face is grave and he huffs as he jabs another into the wet ground. "Sound advice. If given the choice, I would hide."

The mud makes a sucking sound with every rod placed, till the entire pond is encircled like a metal fortress.

Lightning rods. I have read of them. What in the name of Providence are they doing with so many?

"Tell me what you know about her," Brighton growls.

My heartbeat instantly rockets, thrashing against my ribs. Is he enquiring after me?

Jonesy's eyebrows shoot under his jet black hair. "Really? I'm truly astounded. Do you think that inquiry wise?"

Brighton adjusts a pole into the mud as he bites his lip, shaking his head. "No. But I can't seem to help myself, if you must know."

"She has her own set of misfortune, Brighton. And you certainly have…" he stops, his hand indicating the pond in a sweeping gesture, "your own set of woes."

Brighton responds through gritted teeth, "Tell me, Jones."

Their eyes do battle, like two bucks clashing horns.

Finally Jonesy speaks. "No. That is for her to divulge. I will not compromise her trust."

He wants to know my story.

Thrill and fear swell my chest next to bursting.

My head swims and I barely notice as they depart the pond, heading further into the woods. I wrap my arms about myself and pad quietly after them.

They quickly arrive at a barn, the building itself larger than the whole of Brighton's dwelling.

Multi-colored flickering lights dart and dance through the translucent window panes, casting strange shadows across the swamp-grass.

Thunder rumbles a reminder of the impending storm; its vibrations a heavenly tympani in a continuous ethereal drumroll.

It sounds like a warning.

Which I steadfastly ignore.

A mewling makes me startle and trip; my already-tense muscles almost snapping in fear.

Two large cats follow me through the underbrush, their calls growing louder with every step. My head whips between the barn and back; they will give me away with their eerie caterwauling.

"Shh. Shh. You blasted creatures." I crouch down in the ferns, staring them head-on.

One black, one yellow. There is something...*odd* about them. They mewl louder and louder, venturing closer.

"Shh. Shh."

I hold out my hand and the yellow eases his whiskered face to rub against my fingers, then moves to twine his full body against my legs in a feline greeting.

"Oh!"

The black cat leaps onto my lap, kneading my dress, purring as if we were long-lost friends. And I see it. *The paws.*

My blood chills. The paws are far too large, have too many feline toes.

Was there something wrong with these cats?
"Don't be daft."

One of my father's primary complaints was my overactive imagination, to which I had been treated to hours upon hours of lectures.

Of course something was wrong. The better question was, "Are they evil?"

I stare at their furry faces; eager and yearning for affection. *No.* They, too, were lost. Perhaps I belonged here, on this island of curious, lost creatures.

Recognition sneaks around my defenses as I stare at them. Tears burn my eyes and I slump to the ferns.

They remind me of...me.

Images lambast my mind—of myself as a young girl, following my father, *aching* for the slightest inkling of affection. Which never transpired. All embraces and words of comfort died with my mother. Beneath the water.

I think of mother's sketchbook. I have kept it tucked away—the sight of it too much to bear. This morning however, I had unearthed it from the bottom of the armoire and placed it in my pack, resolved to use it. To place my notes alongside her drawings.

I had done so for several hours, and already felt better. I knew it ridiculous, but the thought of her pictures and my music surviving together on the page gave me solace.

A melody fills my head, full of longing and loss, crying to be put to parchment. I opened my pack, caressing my leather-bound book, now rife with my notes.

My sorrows made manifest, each tiny black musical note a smile or a tear.

Jonesy and Brighton's voices rise, and the music in my head fades.

They are arguing. I shove the book back inside my pack and welcome both cats onto my lap, burying my face in their fur, allowing the soothing rhythms of their heartbeats and purrs to lull my pain.

I stay that way for several minutes, catching bits of their squabble, till Jonesy storms out of the barn, stomping through the brush toward the shore.

A shrill *shrieking* erupts from the barn, thickening my blood with fear. Animals screaming for mercy.

In his haste, Jonesy has left the barn door open, allowing the noise to escape onto the night air.

Brighton steps in the doorway, slamming it shut, muting the sound of their pain.

I slide the cats from my lap, fighting to control my rapid breath as I slink toward the window. Was Marietta right?

I don't want to know. I don't want to know.

"You must."

I move slowly toward the barn, and the world seems to slow as I swallow hard.

I drag my hands up the bumpy fieldstone to grasp the windowsill and stand on tip-toes to peer inside.

Two large balls, attached to rods, sit on a wooden table, ridiculously reminding me of metallic dandelions. However to blow on one of these might mean an electrified-death.

Bolts of light leap between the two heads, dancing back and forth, green and red, green and red, as if Brighton somehow captured the lightning from the night sky.

There are no cauldrons, but in their stead are Bunsen burners, with purple, blue and red flames, and various bubbling solutions—so numerous they remind me of Lefroy's lightshow.

A *screeeech* erupts, sprouting gooseflesh up my arms, into my scalp.

My eyes dart across the room.

Animals in cages. Every sort.

Monkeys, cats, dogs, birds. Many *deformed.*

A monkey with an extra limb dangling from its side…a collie with a broken paw limping about its cage. A sparrow with a broken wing frenetically battering against its cage, panic-stricken. My eyes stray back to the monkey. So like a *human.* I have only ever seen one during a visit to the London Zoological Gardens.

What is he doing with them? Did he hurt them?

I stare as Brighton lowers the flame beneath a solution then removes it; placing it with metal tongs onto the rough-hewn table.

69

A rabbit lay beside it on the table, its shallow breathing a prelude of things to come. I shiver, almost feeling death as it hovers, waiting in the room.

My hands clench, and I will myself in place. Not to barge in. *He will not hurt it.* Please do not let him hurt it. *It is so delicate and helpless.*

I raise my hand to wrap on the stained glass at the same moment he takes a dropper and eases four drops of shimmering liquid into the pathetic creature's sagging mouth.

For a moment, nothing. I wonder if he has somehow put it out of its misery. But then—

Furry legs *tap-tap-tap* and almost drum against the table and shoot out straight as the rest of its body quivers like it takes to a palsy.

I hold my breath—my hand poised, still ready to rap the glass.

Its white ears flop and it shakes wildly as if the lightning's current trembles through its furry body.

It *convulses;* ears flapping, as the top layer of skin undulates like some invisible wave laps beneath. And then…

I blink repeatedly and my eyes water from being open wide, so very long.

A myriad of sparkling points, the size of pinpricks, seemingly *burst* through its skin and are gone in the space of time it took me to blink.

My hands cover my mouth in awe and terror. *Have I imagined that?*

The creature rolls and tentatively sits up.

Brighton's face is guarded. Not smiling, not frightened…just cautious.

A hidden someone or *some-thing* shuffles behind

a divider in the back of the room. My breathing puffs out in hard, sharp gasps.

The shape of it is…human. Almost. The man is crooked and bent, like the Magnolia trees swaying in the breeze behind me.

The fireflies arrive, streaking through the air like a trillion-tiny-twinkling bits of stars, fallen from the sky, attaching to his barn

They descend, swarming close to my hand. A few crawl onto my neck and I panic, swatting at them and swear I hear a hiss.

I back away from the window, swiping violently at the air.

"His laboratory. *It is* a laboratory."

I step back further, breathing hard.

Their lighted bodies form a buzzing horde—crawling up the windows, flitting about the roof, teeming on the chimney.

I blink and rub my eyes. The lab winks and twinkles with their eerie luminescence.

I walk backwards, my eyes fixated, my legs tense, preparing for flight if they should alight and descend on *me*.

Something or someone scampers from the other side of the barn. I back up too quickly, stumbling.

Did it spy me?

I feel the ferns brush the back of my leg—I've reached the edge of the woods. The cats leap to the windowsill, meowing and calling back and forth to one and other in a guttural feline symphony.

And then…my heart stops for a tick then surges hard and loud, filling my ears with its beat.

It begins again. The synchronized dot, dot, dash of their sparkling insect bodies. My mind screams with the travesty of nature and I swallow, fighting back tears.

This is significant. I feel it to my core. It is no random event.

A type of communication.

I'd been fascinated by Father's telegraph machine and from an early age, begged, prodded and whined till Monsieur Lafayette, father's chief of security, had sat me down and taught it to me. It was a curious interest for a girl, but he had lost his only daughter to influenza, so I held a particular, singular soft spot in the burly man's heart.

I extract the journal from my bag, watching, repeating and recording the sequences of light, scribbling them down.

Thunder crashes and the first drops of water tap on the top of my head.

In a swirl of black, churning clouds, the storm arrives, dumping buckets of rain into the forest.

I shove the journal back in my bag and turn and dash for the shore.

CHAPTER SEVEN

"How much longer till the Shoot the Chute is completed?" Peter, one of my builders leans over my blueprints, his eyes squinting against the late afternoon sun. We are in the shadow of the guest house, but not enough for his liking.

Silas appointed me my own drawing room within the house, to use for any construction project...but there is an air of malevolence in that building. So I always draw outside, much to Peter's chagrin.

"I would say within a week. Shorter if we had more men."

Silas has been making cuts wherever possible, making his grand projects virtually impossible to complete.

Peter rubs his cheeks, as he does when he is considering. "Do you know any other soul in this God-forsaken place who could lend a hammer?"

I smile slightly. "Perhaps. We're done here, I will check with you at day's end."

Peter nods and tips his hat, "Right." He glances

up at the guest house, "Don't get into any trouble till I see you again. Do you think you can manage that?"

I smile back, "Sometimes trouble needs getting into."

Peter shakes his head, already walking away. "You are a trouble-magnet, LeFroy."

"Indeed."

I stare toward the smattering of tiny cottages, and wonder what she is doing. I have no right to wonder, but I shall just the same.

I try to force out the image of her playing the cello away, but it is seared into my mind like a branding iron. She is utterly breath-taking, of course…but that does not explain the insistent need to be in her presence. I have fought it since the first moment I laid eyes upon her, distancing myself.

My life is so complicated; it would be cruelty to bring her into it. But that does not stop the longing. My mind returns again and again to her faulty finger. It is a minor malady, but it pains me to think on it. I wish to alleviate her suffering…protect her.

I grind my teeth together. "This is not productive. Nor helpful."

I startle and stare around to see if anyone may witness the witch talking to himself. Yet another reason to condemn me. Madness.

I pick up my instrument and stare at it, willing my hand to apply the right amount of force as I touch it to the parchment.

It shatters instantaneously and I curse, whisking it away before ink ruins my work.

I sigh, grind my teeth and extract another.

I stare at the plans, beginning to make changes,

but raised voices from the porch above halt my fingers mid-sketch.

"Officer, I will assure you once again. No such person is employed or has been to Charleston's Fancy." Silas's voice is unnaturally high and formal. If it were not someone of import, I know he would rip the man's head from his shoulders.

I turn and squint. A soldier, by the look of the uniform, stands nose to nose with Silas.

I gather up the drawing and retreat closer to the house, out of sight, but still within earshot.

"My Lord will pay you for any and all information pertaining to this person."

"I understand. If I see or have a patron matching your description, I assure you I shall be in touch."

Worry tickles the back of my throat. *Is it she?*

I must find the story of her past. My longing rears its head excitedly—that I must now speak to her. Must find out.

I gather my belongings and press my lips together. This must be handled carefully.

I am spying. Once again. A common voyeur. My mother always warned that my curiosity must be curbed. *What is it about LeFroy?*

I have been enamored before, of course, with local boys whom Father immediately forbid me from seeing; for fear they would distract *me* from my music, and *he* from his primary asset. Also my music.

A revelation strikes and a shiver courses my spine. *LeFroy makes me forget my music.*

For a time anyway. That has never, ever happened before.

The notes, the tones, the stories I weave into the sound have long been my respite from the suffocation that is the real, crushing world.

Despite his aloof nature, despite his oft-surly words, something about the slight upturn of his mouth, the hint of playfulness in his words, betray there is much more to him. A kinder self. That he is steadfastly hiding. From me and from the world at large.

I step off the thoroughfare and into the woods, despite Silas's ardent warnings, and head in the direction of the Shoot-the-Chute. I first came across it the other day when I decided to try to find the drawings in mother's book.

She was fascinated with sketching bodies of water. Both here, in Charleston, every place I ever played, and in our homeland.

I happened on the Shoot the Chute, half-completed, several weeks prior.

I have practiced my excuse for searching him out; we still have two more shows to compose. Only one is finished.

Brighton has been steadfastly avoiding me, and if I wish to see him, I know I have a choice of three locales; the shoot, the gradual lighting of the Guest House, or the isle.

My mind replays the rabbit spectacle from the other eve. *Did he heal that rabbit?* It was a breath from death. I bite my lip.

LeFroy is engineer, electrician and resident master of pyrotechnics.

He is not, however, an apostle, able to resurrect the dead.

The man is obviously brilliant. "And obviously trouble," I whisper.

My eyes steal to the night sky, clear as the toll of the church's bell, and intuitively know if the dusk is cloudless, he toils somewhere, carrying out the business of Charleston's Fancy. If the night were stormy, I would no doubt find him on the rocky isle.

His soul is restless. I have never seen him still for more than a moment.

When he sat transfixed by my music was the only time I've seen the veil over his features lift. But I was too transported by my own notes to stop.

The scraping of saws and of axes hitting trees reaches my ears. I head in a straight line toward the sound, taking care to slink behind the thick overgrown trees.

The brush thins into a clearing and I see Brighton and...I squint. *Jonesy?* Whatever is Jones about? I took Jones for a musician, only—not a laborer?

Behind them is the Shoot-the-Chute, almost complete by the look of it. My eyes steal across it; a long stairway climbs the back to the tallest tower I have ever seen, where passengers may wait beneath a roof for the ride of their life.

My eyes jump down the greased boards where the boat will plummet and *splash* into the sound and my heart immediately pounds with fear at the prospect.

I am not fond of heights.

"How many more, Brighton?" Jones calls, startling me.

I ease myself behind the tree till only my eyes peak around.

"Why, you tiring out on me friend?" Brighton's tone teases.

Jonesy wipes his forehead, and halts chopping the massive tree he's apparently going to fell. "I can go as long as you. Longer. Just wondering so I can pace myself—"

Craaak!

My head whips to the sky, searching for lightning. Nothing. Still clear.

Craaak!

The tree lurches left. But there's no wind?

The trunk splits.

"Jones!"

The next moments blur. Brighton bounds across the clearing, leaps over the downed logs and is over Jones before I've had time to bellow a warning.

The tree is sailing towards his head. Jones dives to the dirt, but his legs are still in its crushing path.

And somehow. I blink, shaking my head, my heart vibrating my ribs with the staccato beat— Brighton stands over Jonesy.

The tree *slams* across his shoulders, buckling his knees, sinking his feet ankle-deep into the clay, and I cry out—instantly covering my traitor-mouth.

I hurry toward them, forgetting myself.

The trunk snaps in half as it strikes his shoulders, the top half heading towards Jonesy's head.

"Jones!" he screams again.

Jonesy's eyes widen and he rolls right as the evergreen top collapses so close an outlying branch slashes his face.

Brighton pitches off the massive trunk, sending it flying, *no cartwheeling*, as if it he were flicking a bloody matchstick.

He extends his hand to Jonesy, still supine on the ground.

They clasp hands and soon Jones is righted, vigorously dusting mud and wood from his trousers.

Joney's eyes narrow. "That was entirely too close. Apparently I shall not trade my violin for the lumberjack circuit."

Brighton pulls him into a quick, fierce hug and releases him. "No, my friend. No more felling trees for you."

I come to my senses just as I've reached the forest threshold, one more step and I will be starkly visible in the moonlight and lanterns.

Chest heaving, I lean against the tree, waiting.

Jonesy's gaze is serious, but does not match the wild fear and awe I feel pinching my own.

That blow would've, nay should've, killed *any* man. Yet here he stands.

My conscious whispers, 'Witchcraft'.

I shake my head, willing away the words.

"You weren't exaggerating," Jones says, bending to pick up his axe.

Brighton's face is grim. "No. I wish I were. But it certainly came in useful today, no matter how odious its origins."

"Sorry about the tree." Jones says sheepishly. "It has been awhile since I left the farm."

"Not to worry my friend." Brighton's eyes are sweeping the forest line and I take another step backward, fear filling my mouth.

"What is it?" Jones says, his posture immediately shifting to attention.

Brighton's eyebrow rises. "I don't know. Never you mind. Let's finish this."

I spin and bound through the thicket, ignoring the tear and hot sting of thistles against my arms.

LeFroy really may be a witch.

And my friend, my very dear friend, is a party to it.

I cluck to the horse, and angle her down the cobblestones, heading toward the bay and the shipyards. The customs house, situated at the pinnacle of a very long stretch of road, I suspect was no accident. It's message; all roads lead to commerce here in Charleston.

The sky is a clear, cloudless blue and the clops of the mare's feet are attempting to lull me into security. But I will not hear of it.

Vexation is as much a part of me as breathing, this I have come to accept as my newfound reality.

But recently, worry and angst have thwarted any other emotion that used to reside inside me.

My mind is full of her once again. This may be my greatest vexation. I need my mind to be focused. It is selfish to want her.

I have done something despicable, completely unthinkable. I have eavesdropped on Allegra, fabricated reasons to be in her proximity.

As I worked on arc lamps, I have heard her teaching her charges to play. She was so utterly kind to all of her students. So patient. There is no falsehood in her.

My mother once said, Judge a person by the way they treat those who can do nothing for them.

Allegra's heart beats true. Too true. This world is not a place for the kind. Her goodness reminds me of George.

I run my fingers roughly through my hair and grip the reins tighter. My mind breaks free of my careful self-control—releasing an onslaught of images through my mind; I wish to know everything about her. To touch her, to never have her out of my sight. To protect her. My heart stops when I see her...

"For the love of all that is holy. You are a lost cause," I murmur.

I grind my teeth and force my wits to the task at hand.

My shipment of chemicals, necessary for the oh-so-vital pyrotechnic, should've arrived weeks ago. But with the political climate...with talk of succession, impending war, shipments had been late, if arriving at all.

As the carriage rattles by the local pub, my eye is drawn to the multi-colored flyers; advertisements are plastered all about the windows.

One is for Charleston's Fancy. *Orchestra! Moonlight! Magnificent!*

A faded poster titled, *Come See Miss Mary Marvel-The musical crown-jewel of Europe. One Night Only.*

My eyes skip across several others and click back as my breath catches.

"Brighton." I cock my head, confused. Someone calls again, "*Brighton!*"

My head quickly swivels away from the advertisements. Indeed I cluck to the horses, putting as much space between me and them as possible.

Silas. Perfect.

"Whoa." I tug on the reins and the team halts before him, his white walking stick swinging.

I have it on authority from local slaves that stick has everything to do with caning and naught to do with walking.

Silas steps toward the carriage, his hand raised in greeting. "What brings the *mysterious* Monsieur LeFroy to the glorious port of Charleston this day?" He flutters his fingers mockingly.

"Your pyrotechnics. And you had better pray the shipment has arrived or your new production will be decidedly less colorful." I grind my teeth together.

"Ah. Well, good. I shan't detain you then. Commerce must commence. And more importantly, the show must go on." Silas steps away, heading toward the water, walking stick swinging jauntily at his side.

I cluck and the team ambles forward. When they try to break into a trot, knowing the water is their destination I pull back on the reins to slow their pace, waiting till Silas's back disappears into the customs building.

"Whoa." I flip the reins around a hitching post and vault from the seat, striding down the street as quickly as I can manage without drawing undue attention.

"Mam. Sir," I say genially, tipping my hat, weaving my way past townsfolk, my eyes fixated on the poster. With a sideways glance, I snatch it from the window, fold it and stuff it into my waistcoat pocket.

Hurrying back to the team, my breath is coming hard and fast as I slide into the driver's bench.

As each fold opens, dread seeps thicker and thicker into my mouth.

Have you seen this woman?

Missing. Miss Katherine Manners, Cellist and Musical Prodigy.

Miss Manners was last seen performing in the state of South Carolina.

Reward via Lord Lawrence Manners for her safe return to her loving family.

Contact local authorities with any information.

Unmistakable doe-brown eyes stare back.

Allegra's eyes, from beneath an elaborate hairstyle of upswept strawberry-blonde locks.

Her fingers tightly clutch the neck of a cello, a sad smile on her wide, full lips.

I dab my forehead as the light sheen of sweat breaks out.

I scan the whole street, fervently searching for more pamphlets.

Allegra

"Alright Tom. You practice now. I shall see you later so that you may assist me."

The boy's wide smile is infectious.

"Of course. Thank you so much, mam."

He steps out of my cottage and onto the thoroughfare, heading back towards the hustle and bustle of Charleston's Fancy.

The nod and tip of his hat is so utterly adult. The orphan boy has stolen my heart completely.

He turns to go, and I bite the inside of my lip. *Did his limp seem less pronounced today?*

That was impossible. Club feet did not mend. The cry of a gull shifts my attention to the sea.

Tom, too, is a slave to the park. Silas recently began '*taking in strays*' as he called them. Seeming to altruistically adopt orphans, providing them room and board—but I have seen how he works them. I swallow the disgust thickening my throat.

The morning is clear and bright; the white clouds a fluffy contrast against the baby-blue sky. The breeze puffs in off the bay like hot, salty breath, tickling my hair across my cheek. In the distance I see the red striped poof that is the aerial balloon. I have never dared to alight in one. I am frightened of heights, but the playful bob and weave of it in the breeze, make me wish I was not.

I stroll out into the thoroughfare, breathing deep, filling my lungs with the air's salty tang. It is early; only men readying the amusements are about. Sarah was up and gone before the sun arose. Silas keeps her bustling each day until the very hour she collapses into bed each night.

My eyes stray across the bay…to the rock-mass beyond.

White gulls swarm the rocks, dipping and diving to the water's surface and soaring back up as they fish.

I have strategically avoided the isle for a week; steadfastly refusing to admit why.

For instance, ignorance is bliss?

After seeing such tremendous strength, how he

discarded a tree-trunk as if flicking a matchstick—my nights have been plagued with dreams of him performing endless feats of strength. They culminated last night in him dressed in a strong-man's uniform from the carnival.

I smile and cover my lips. It is not a matter for jest, I know. It should vex me more than it does. If I was any other girl, I would've told every person I know.

I couldn't even bring myself to tell Sarah, for fear it might somehow convict him.

It was madness. Completely out of my character—but for once, I truly didn't care. My heart seemed to beat in my chest *for him.*

For the moments he regarded me.

When I held his attention, I felt *alive*. Like all things were possible.

It felt…like when I play my music. I swallow with the realization.

Nothing or no-one has ever come close to matching that feeling. The soaring-wonder that fills my soul.

The icy enclosure that keeps my heart in a perpetual winter and hibernation is thawing. I feel the hot stirrings of life within and a renewed beat of hope surging through my veins.

My whole life has been self-denial. Hiding my thoughts, my true feelings.

He does not demand that, nay he discourages it.

I know how rare and precious love to be. And I, like a miser, *must have it.*

"Lost in thought, are we?"

I looked up, realizing in horror I've arrived back at the Shoot-the-Chute. The scene of the crime.

The park staff has been buzzing about its opening for weeks. The talk was that Brighton had designed it after riding the first-ever chute in Watchtower Park, Illinois.

I step back, admiring his handiwork close up. The towering wooden ramp, built into a hillside, now housed a large boat, precariously positioned at the top.

"Like what you see?"

Brighton is on the steps, his grin so wide and contagious, I cannot help but return it. I blush at his double entendre. It is the other Brighton. The carefree one.

I nod. "Yes. It's amazing."

He rolls his eyes as if this hulking contraption were a mere house of cards, built solely for his amusement. "It's nothing, a distraction from life. It is, however, ready."

His eyes sparkle like a child's. My breath catches and holds, but my brow furrows with confusion. I wonder how long this altogether different Brighton shall stay?

"It is ready?"

"Come take a ride." He thrusts out his hand. "Or should I say, a plunge?"

"I." My eyes shoot up, and I lick my lips, taking in the height, the greased wooden track. I envision the boat barnstorming the slide and shake my head. "I don't know."

He steps down and gently extricates my hand from where it is adhered to my side.

"Ouch!" I quickly withdraw my hand from his.

His eyebrows knit. "Whatever is the matter?"

I shake my hand vigorously. I don't wish to

admit my weakness, but his direct stare searches my body for injuries and I flush.

I reluctantly extend my hand. "My. My index finger. I have been playing so much, what with my music lessons, and the new symphonies. I believe I may have injured it."

He reaches down and snatches my hand without permission, his gaze ticking back and forth over my digits and palm. My first finger, which undoubtedly endures the most abuse when I play, is noticeably swollen.

He nods. "Aye. I have something for that, but don't have it on my person."

He releases my hand and my heart hammers hard against my ribs.

"In the meantime, come take a ride. It will get your mind off it." His voice is so playful; I feel the quiver of a smile breaking through...until I glance upward.

I stare up; taking in the full, dizzying height of the structure and my heart takes flight in my chest as my feet ache to do the same.

As if hearing its protestations, he says, "Don't be daft, girl. You will love it. I promise."

He pulls me up the stairs, shuffling me in front of him—trapping me with his arms. I'm quite sure so I could not flee.

In my mind, I hear the snap and splitting of the tree as it struck his shoulders.

Indeed, if Brighton wished to detain me, there would be naught I could do to stop him.

My boot falls echo on the steps and we rise higher and higher; my heart seeming to mimic our ascent in its journey toward my mouth.

A group of Charleston's Fancy employees, both men and women, wait at the top, chattering and tittering with excitement.

I chance a glance over the side and my stomach flips. "Are you quite certain this is safe?"

He pulls me close, too close for convention, and leans forward to whisper in my ear. The tingle on my chest ignites like his many fireworks.

His scent consumes me, and my eyelids drift half-shut.

His stubble grazes my cheek. "I would *never* put you at risk. You are safe with me. No matter the place."

If I only turn my head, I may taste his lips.

He pulls back with a wistful half-smile but his eyes are deadly serious.

"Oy, Brighton. Quit mucking about. We haven't all day—we aren't the bloody patrons ye know."

A curvy blond adds, "Yes, do hurry Brighton. Silas will roll our heads down this track instead of your lovely little boat."

Brighton turns with a wicked grin and hauls me up the steps, into the crowd.

One by one we clamber into the wide boat.

Brighton and I slide…into the front row.

I peek over the edge and panic surges, closing my throat. Vertigo tilts my vision and I jam my eyes shut.

It was a *very* long way down. I'd only ever been so high on the Ferris wheel at the Great Exposition.

Brighton slides closer. I try to focus on the feel of his thigh against mine, ignoring the river of fear flooding my mouth. He feels abnormally warm, as if a fever courses through his veins.

He reaches across me, pulling a leather strap across my lap, his lap, and the two others seated beside us. It secures by a metal hitch into the opposite wall of the boat.

"Oh, my word," the fair-haired girls squeaks behind me.

I blink, surprised to see Tom, my student, next to Brighton, tugging on the strap. "Can I do it again, after this first one?"

Brighton laughs out loud. "We'll see, lad."

Excited murmurs escalate into shouts.

A crowd gathers at the bottom of the shoot. I search through it till I spy Sarah and Jonesy's upturned faces. Their expressions match the cloying clench of fear in my chest. Sarah reaches out to clutch Jonesy's forearm and his hand drapes over hers.

Brighton whispers silkily, "Steady, love. All is well."

Then he turns, with a boisterous bark, "Alright James, let 'er fly, just as we practiced."

James stares down at the crowd and on seeing Silas, clears his throat.

Silas paces at the bottom like an expectant father. My hair on my nape rises like hackles. *Money.* I know he pictures the chute as a towering stack of potential coin in lieu of wood and stairs and sweat.

He stares at the shoot, his hands rubbing together so furiously, I fear they might smoke and alight. His infamous cane is cast to the ground, forgotten for the moment.

Leave it to that man to cheapen such an experience.

"Ladies and gentlemen, you are about to witness

the maiden voyage of the *Runaway,* Charleston's first Shoot-the-Chute amusement. It was conceived by our fair owner, Silas, and brought to life by Mr. LeFroy. Without further ado."

James tips his hat and motions to the men to slide the boat forward.

The nose tips and I smell the grease-lined track.

"Oh-my-word-oh-my-word—"

Brighton's voice in my ear, "Relax, love." His arm presses reassuringly behind my back, securing me tight against his side. "Don't resist."

My mind reels and I bite back the response, *You? Or the ride?*

The boat rocks and teeters and *plummets.* Sliding and growling as the bottom hums against the track.

We are free-falling.

My stomach leaps to my throat and crashes back to my guts in a single exhale. My hair streams from my face and my lips crack into a broad smile.

"That's it," Brighton croons.

For a glorious, brief moment I forget. Forget my father, forget the soldier, forget to fear.

Vibration hums the seat beneath my bottom as the boat pelts forward down the track.

Cheers erupt behind us from the platform then spread through the waiting crowd below like a wave of jubilation.

The boat's nose connects with a jolt and a splash and a deluge sweeps over the front, dowsing us through.

I am laughing.

Harder than I can ever remember.

Happiness *surges* through me, watering my eyes.

"That, is what freedom feels like." Brighton

smiles and his eyes are full of meaning. *Did he mean my freedom? The northern aggression?*

"Brighton! Brighton! Look here!"

His eyes leave mine, but the smile remains.

A cheer erupts, "Hooray for the Runaway!"

Silas beams as he leads the cry again, his walking stick poking at the sky.

And the revelation strikes; the name of the boat.

He named it after me...he knows.

I swallow, trying to master my breathing as they steer the boat back toward the launch.

Chapter Eight

I make my way across the grass to the gazebo, still wringing the water out of my dress. It seems the smile is now a permanent fixture of my face. I keep trying to remove it, but my muscles seem set in joy.

I slide to my orchestra seat, barely noticing anything or anyone, still stuck in the rapture of my imagination; where the feel of Brighton's arm and his murmurs in my ear repeat, over and over like a velvety chorus.

Jonesy takes his place beside me, his dark complexion looking somehow sallow today. I fear for his health, but before I might enquire, Plimpton taps for attention, and several musicians make their way up to his podium.

He hands out the sheet music and bestows on me a wide smile and I beam back.

He does not hand me a copy. I've seen it once, that is sufficient.

All my mind needs. My father called it, *'photographic'*.

I call it natural as breathing.

The music dances across my mind—a musical vision, accompanied by every note, chord and major and minor.

What a glorious day. A ride with Brighton, and now new music.

I grin like a fool at Jonesy and his face becomes even more grave. My lips finally falter.

"Well, what is it? Out with it. I see you are determined to ruin my day."

"I...found the document for the Morse Code."

I'd given Jones my notes on the blinking lights from the island. Despite my best attempts I could not remember all of the code. My instructor would be so disappointed.

Gooseflesh erupts, tingling from my scalp to my bottom. I swallow. "Go on."

Other musicians brush past me, momentarily blocking Jonesy's pinched face. I lean backward to permit them passage. It is as if time elongates; my heart beating harder with every stretched, waiting moment.

I still see, the patterned twinkling, repeating over and again, like a musical *ostinato*—a repeated phrase throughout a song.

Mercifully, after the sounds of chairs shifting and petticoats settling I am finally permitted to stare into Jonesy's dark, serious face once again.

His lips quiver in a way I've never seen. Percival Jones, though small in stature, has the largest, most courageous heart I've ever seen. A warrior's heart.

His distress is contagious and my throat thickens with fear.

"The light's pattern spelled, stay away." He shakes his head. "*Repeated* stay away."

My hands fly to cover my mouth, but were too late to stop my sharp intake of breath.

He jams the tiny book into my shaking hands. "What is this?"

"Morse Code. You best hold onto that. For translation."

Jonesy swallows, and plunges on, "I saw you with him today. I see how you look at him, Allegra. He is…my friend, my very good friend, tis true. But even *I* do not understand how *this* is possible."

I press my lips so tight they hurt. The cats, the lightning, the rods, his inhuman strength…*the crooked man.*

I think of the sparkle in his eyes as he playfully hauled me up the steps of the shoot. Could that have been mere hours ago? It now seems a lifetime.

"I refuse to believe he is evil."

Jonesy grips my forearm, squeezing it hard, demanding my gaze.

"I did not say he was evil. But he has…" Jones eyes are wild, looking everywhere but into mine. "He has many serious problems. And you have your own."

A rebellious flush spreads across my chest. "I care not. I—"

Jones cuts across me. "The last line said, stay away, *Allegra.*"

Brighton

94

"Tom, do come here."

The small boy hurries from the kitchen, drying his hands on the front of his trousers. "Aye, sir."

His club foot slows his progress, but he arrives at my side as quickly as he is able. "Are you certain you wish to try again? You truly understand the risks, my boy?"

He nods fervently. I feel the heat rise from my collar and I pace before him. He may be only twelve, but his nomadic, orphan-existence has hardened and matured his mindset. Indeed, staring into his eyes is nothing like staring into Lucy's.

Lucy. I blink as guilt flits about my head, trying to form a chip on my already laden shoulder. Best not think on her.

"I understand Mr. LeFroy. But be honest. How am I to get work like this?" His hand sweeps to his foot. "Mr. Silas pays me, but it's just enough to survive sir. And he will never increase it. He will keep me tied to him till I'm as old as Bartholomew."

I knew it to be true. Every blasted word of it. *More guilt.* I should take Tom away. I'd offered, and he'd stoutly refused, stating he was separated from his younger sister when his parents had passed from smallpox. He was certain she was nearby and refused to leave without her.

I swallow the lump threatening in my throat. The boy has more courage than most men I know.

I sigh. "This is completely, utterly against my better judgment, but seeing as how you stole the first batch—"

"I'm sorry, sir. But I saws what it did to 'em rabbits sir, so I just *had* to try—"

"Enough." I slip the bottle into his calloused palm. "Two drops, not a tad more. I'll not do it. You will have to do it yourself."

My stomach turns at the hopeful smile on his face. "Yes, sir."

"Do not forget my warning. What it is capable of, if abused."

He plucks it from the table and begins to shuffle into the next room. "I won't sir. I'll do just as you instruct."

"Remember *two drops*. Heed my words, boy. I'm going out, Tom. I'll return directly."

His eyes steal to the rain, battering the window. "In this weather, sir?"

I close the door on his inquiry and flip up the collar of my coat against the driving rain.

The lightning blazes and my gaze shoots out to the sea, only barely visible through the break in the thick isle vegetation.

A center bolt, raw and blazing-blue strikes the water *again* and *again*, while electrified tendrils shoot out on every side as if it seeks to expand its reach.

"One, two, three, four," I whisper. *Not enough voltage.*

I hear the feline caterwauling begin in the forest and glance behind in time to see the predictable swarm of fireflies alighting from a thick Oak.

Craaack! The sky lights as if the angels wage a heavenly battle.

I jog faster, sloshing my way through the ferns and underbrush. A branch dislodges and I leap

96

over it, running full-on toward the pond. Toward him.

Mud forms and I skid to a halt, almost colliding with the lightning rods.

Craack!

My eyes shoot skyward as the black blustery clouds part to permit a cascading heavenly downpour.

The thick bolt flashes, illuminating the pond and clearing in a luminescent blue, so that for single moment, night is day. *Is it day where he is?*

A silence, a mere beat and—"Good word!" I step backward, fighting to catch my breath.

From the storm's center a violent flash erupts. A fiery string of lightning slashes the dark like a sizzling whip-crack and *connects* to the pole before me, setting it humming and vibrating.

The current quivers and leaps across the rods, one by one, forming undulating thick plasma, like a comet's tail.

"Yes. Yes! Go you bloody monster!"

The current races about the circle, till it reaches the initial contact-rod and a field forms— translucent and cloudy-blue, like some bizarre, electrified candy-floss.

The surface of the pool ripples and bubbles. Images whisk across it. Tears fill my eyes. "Thank Providence. Finally. *Finally.*"

I step *into* the current, barely feeling the sting and the smell of burning hair on my arms. For a few long moments, I levitate, stuck between this reality and the next.

The current spits me out and I fall to my knees before the water, plunging my hand into the foam.

The images, *people*, blink and shimmer on the surface.

The cats stalk beside the pond, ten in all, circling the perimeter of blue floss, crying out to one another as the fireflies hover above the water, dipping and almost, but not quite touching the bubbling surface.

The racing pictures slow, and halt. *And he is there*.

"George," I choke. "Oh, Georgie. I'm so sorry."

The pond skates through time like a revolving roulette wheel. I need it to halt and hold on where George is *now*. Not the ruddy past.

He is only twelve; his brown innocent eyes stared up trustingly at my father, who brandishes a syringe toward his extended arm. My throat closes, "Oh, Georgie."

Anger burns every beat of my heart. *That I was not there. Did not stop him.*

The images shift once again, and my chest contracts with the pain.

George and Lucy, down by the bay. Lucy is tiny, perhaps three.

George bolts after her, playing tag. George, at five, could not speak. Had only his hands to communicate.

Lucy toddles towards a bridge, half-submerged in the swamp.

George's eyes widen and he dashes ahead of her, standing before the entrance, arms spread wide, not letting her pass.

He inhales deeply, "Help!"

The hot stings of tears course my face. *His first word*. His first word uttered protecting his sister.

Providence, he is so good. Why did he not take me?

A shifting of images again.

George *now*. Yes. It is he, *now*. Where I wish to be, where I *need* to be.

Simple, kind, adult George, with...someone I've never seen before.

A tall, blonde beauty. She holds out her hand to him. My heart sears with pain.

A minion sent by my horrible father?

His face gives way into a huge smile as she slides her thin hand into his thick one.

How can this be? The George I know is like a child. Not capable of...love between a man and woman?

Something about his face; an awareness in his eyes, I have not seen since his childhood, since the accident left his mind wanting.

My brow furrows and panic and rage pump through my veins.

"George!" I scream, knowing he cannot hear me.

I pause. The hesitation is not more than a few beats of my heart-but with each pulse in my ear, I see *her*. My desire and need and...love for her, hold me back.

I hurtle off the bank and dive. Cold and heat rush past and envelope the length of my body like sinus waves. I open my eyes under the water. To utter blackness. I am too late.

I swim upward, kicking, bursting through the surface, searching furiously left and right.

"No! *No*."

A still pond. Deadened, lifeless silver poles. No current.

No images.

The storm moved on. And has taken with it, my heart.

The dream drives me from my bed once again. My mother, surrounded by Magnolias, dripping in them. They spread before her like a flowery path and when she begins to speak, fetid water, laden with white petals pours from her dead, open mouth.

I sit up, trying to catch my breath. My eyes steal across the room to Sarah's door and I stifle the sobs.

If she hears me, she will no doubt comfort me, without any regard for her own fatigue. She has been by my side, holding my hand, through a countless number of these recurring dreams since my mother's demise.

As many as I permit her to see.

My eyes flick back without my permission to my mother's sketchbook and my hand reaches for it of its own accord. I hug it tightly and slide to the bed's edge.

Mother died here, in Charleston, the first time we visited.

I shudder as the images flicker across my mind like a black-and-white photodrama.

It was our second tour to the States, and mother had been so excited, without a trace of the melancholy which so often plagued her.

I can still feel her hands in my curls, arranging my hair; her dark eyes staring gravely overtop the pile to pierce me in the mirror.

"Play well, tonight Allegra," she said seriously.

"There is something…amazing about this place. I feel it. If they like your music, perhaps they shall ask us back again."

And she smiled so widely, I couldn't help but believe it.

But it did not end that way. We came back, but without her.

She chose this place, over me. The lump in my throat clogs my breathing and I press my lips tighter, my fingernails biting into the sketchbook's cover.

That is why I chose *here* to flee Father's yoke. To somehow, someway be closer to her. Or what was left of her, lost somewhere to the waters.

I try in vain to shut the memory-door, but I've carelessly cracked it open and the images slip out.

My father, his face red with rage, shaking all over, brandishes my mother's parasol like a sword as I peer through the crack in the door. "She is *gone*," he roared.

His first officer, Mr. Barrow, shook his head. "Sir?"

"This is all that is bloody well left." He shakes it in his face. "The lunatic drowned herself."

I slam and bolt the memory closed, my hands and body shaking around her sketchbook, still clutched to my chest.

Madness lies in remembering.

I throw off the coverlet and pad toward the cottage door, sliding my bare feet into my boots as I hastily throw a day dress over my shoulders and wrestle it down to my knees.

I rush into the night, blinking to clear the blur of tears. The bright white moon comes into focus and lights my steps.

Mother's horribly abrupt departure from my life; could it only have been two years prior?

For me, my mother's death has altered time's hourglass; in one moment, it seems only yesterday she was smiling and clapping, but if I reflect on all the events that have transpired since her passing—it seems a millennium.

I clasp the book tighter, one of my few tangible proofs of her existence.

There is some light along Fancy's walkways, lanterns set ablaze for the security force. I pick up my pace; wanting to avoid the scolding I will undoubtedly receive if one of the guards happens upon me.

I am a treasured piece of china, once again— trading father for Silas.

But again, not treasured for myself. For my music. It is always for my music.

How I might line another's pocket.

I stop beneath one of the lanterns and flip through the sketchbook and locate the picture.

Mother had even drawn a crude map with a playful X, marking the spot. Two recurring themes are found within my mother's sketches.

The first being, *water.* Ponds, tide pools, waterfalls, the sea, rivers.

And then, beneath each drawing, is a tiny mystery.

My mother very curiously sketched either a window or a tiny ornate door below each body of water.

Some have magnolias, my mother's favorite flower, dangling all about the pools in white, silky clumps. So true to life, I can almost smell their cloying sweetness drifting from the page.

For two years this riddle has driven me mad.

What did it mean?

My mother was nothing but pragmatic. I have no doubt the riddle was intended for me. And me alone.

Thus began my obsession with locating and visiting every body of water that had poured out of her talented fingertips.

She had never let me see her sketchbook as a child, and I know this too is significant, as surely as I feel the thrum of my heart. I flick my fingertips, a nervous habit left-over from childhood, which drove my father mad.

I smile and flick them all the harder.

I hurry to the shore and walk quickly, whisking along the tree line.

A movement catches my eye and my heart flutters in fear of discovery. I adhere myself to an ancient oak to peek around.

A violent geyser surges upward like a frothing-white, upside-down waterfall as the incoming tide collides into the rocky shore.

The burning on my chest lights and I scratch at the skin beneath my pendant.

The tide pool. Just as mother depicted in her book.

I *run* and in minutes am staring down into its depths, my eyes constantly flicking to the surf, minding the return of high tide.

Orange sea-stars and scuttling crabs of every

color litter the bowl and my breath catches and I choke, "Momma. Why. *How* could you leave me with him?"

I sit on the bowl's edge, taking care of the slippery stones and flip the book open.

Below the picture, my finger slides down to caress the tinier picture.

If there was any doubt as to what it was, beside it, in her elegant script, is the word, *Window*.

I whisper the word, bending close to the water and it…ruffles. Like a breeze has blown across it.

I feel my eyebrow arch and I scramble to stand as another wave hits, sending a volcano of seawater into the air. I bite my lip as the cold water droplets shower me…and say it again. "*Window*."

The water darkens, and the sea creatures disappear, melting away from view. The burning on my chest is excruciating, and I lurch forward but I cannot, will-not, draw my eyes away.

Images glide across the top like ice skater's on a winter pond.

I squint, my hands covering my face and my open mouth.

Is there a connection with Brighton's pond? But *it* had something to do with the silver rods. Is *this* what he seeks at the water's edge?

I have no rods, so why is it happening here?

A burly man, with arms like small tree-trunks, slams a hammer over and over again. *A Smith. He's a smithy.*

He's sitting now, staring through an eyepiece, molding something very small, very delicate.

A woman's skirt is barely in view, but I make out the fine lace of its hem, though she is not fully visible. The image is like a moving photo, and she stands just at its border.

Thunder rumbles overhead and the images falter.

My mind grapples with the puzzle, but it's just out of reach like the fading remnants of a dream. *My chest.* My chest is burning, itching—I bite down on my lip to stifle the cry.

"No. Please, I don't understand." Panic tightens my throat as if my mother is in reach and an empty hole in my soul opens, that I will lose her once again.

"Please!" I shriek, forgetting myself, forgetting the nearby security. The shrillness of my cry raises gooseflesh on my arms.

Thunder again. Lightning flashes. The images flicker and die.

I jam mother's sketchbook beneath my dress and flee toward the tree line and…remember.

The lace. Beyond that lace, to the right, was a Magnolia patch.

That was the hem of my mother's skirt.

One week later
Allegra

The heat on the veranda is stifling and I flutter my fan, though I know it to be futile.

I stare and shuffle, marveling that a mere porch could be so very beautiful. I stare over the porch rail into a man-made Eden. Crepe myrtles and palmettos give the illusion of water on land as their fronds whisper and flutter in the salty breeze. Pink azaleas dot the stone walkways and magnolias flower and bloom at every turn.

Silas's ornate privacy door which leads to the midway is closed. People pass by; I see them, coming and going about their business, but not a one dares to glance up at us.

I'd learned the hard way about the Southern custom; when one's door was closed, it meant the occupants were not ready to receive guests, despite the fact the owners might be clearly visible from the street on their open porch. Southerners considered it the *height* of rudeness to disrespect this custom.

One man, Tom, perhaps a foreigner like me, had ignored this crucial rule, gawking as some well-to-doers lounging on their *piazza*. He was promptly *jailed*...and earned the name, Peeping Tom.

Silas considers me, breaking my reverie; his black eyes rove boldly without the slightest regard for propriety.

I flush deeply and quickly hand him my symphony, fighting to keep my hand steady. The man *smells* weakness; imbibes and swallows and distills it for his own personal use. My heart picks up to a staccato rhythm, as it always does in his presence; which has naught to do with attraction and everything to do with survival.

Being in his presence is like dancing around a jungle cat. One false word or move, and he will pounce.

His face brightens as he scans the notes. "Marvelous. I assume you've penned a copy for Mr. Plimpton?"

I automatically nod. *He is tone deaf, what does he know of marvelous?* I stifle the grin at his choice of words.

I should be thrilled. My *first* original score—and an entire orchestra will play it.

My finger throbs; a physical manifestation of all my hours of composition and practice. I fight not to flex my fingers, to give Silas any indication I may be a liability.

Beneath my skirt, my legs twitch, anxious to vacate the piazza. Wild thoughts fill my head.

There is a certain madness to Silas. That he seems to give free reign when I am alone with him.

His nostrils flare as he stares out across the garden. I recognize lust when it's before me. Father paraded a fair share of suitors, all tight as thoroughbreds, ready to bed me in a word.

Fear that he will *take me* right here, right now, regardless of the passing workers is a distinct possibility. *Daring* them to glance up. To do something about it, if they dare.

Sweat pops on my brow and my fan flutters in response.

"Will you not stay?" He gestures to the lunch of fresh mussels, laid upon an ornate silver tray on the serving table.

My skin prickles, thinking of the rash that will ensue if I touch even one.

"No, thank you, sir. I must make haste. Practice, you know."

He is beside me in a blink. My hands grip the piazza railing and I fight the swoon borne of fear.

His finger wraps about my curl as he purrs,

107

"Allegra. You are a most peculiar creature. Peculiar, but oh so enticing."

I swallow and inch away from him but he closes the gap once again.

I hear a girlish giggle from the street below and feverishly wish myself there, inside that girl's body and life, *my* voice issuing that innocent sound.

Silas plants his lips in the small space below my ear and whispers, "I shall have you. One way or the other. Wouldn't it be simpler to just consent. I will even give you the honor of becoming my bride."

I shudder as his fingers splay and trail down my neck which burns red-hot.

"I do not think so—"

"Do, remember, *sweet* Allegra, that soldiers search the streets for you this very night, and all it would take is a singular word from me to sending you packing."

I shift tactics. "I am, of course, highly honored by such a suggestion and proposal, sir." My face blushes hot with the lie, but he seems to be even more enamored by the color.

My breath is coming faster and I struggle to hide it.

I choose my words carefully—he is a powder-keg of a man, and my words the ignition.

"I." I clear my throat to vanquish the fear. "I am so very honored, Mr. Boone..." I step toward the exit, never dropping our gaze. "But I need to focus on my music. I am a savant of sorts, unable to properly divide my attentions..."

I have reached the door; I jump as the doorknob rattles against my back.

His smile is lascivious. A jackal licking his lips.

"Of course. I can see how I might become your obsession; distract you from your music. Which we both need. But one day, I fear my need for you, shall supersede even my need for the coin your music provides."

I curtsy and hurry out the privacy door, my heart hammering against my ribs so hard I feel the impending swoon, but breathe deeply through my nose and out my mouth to ward it off.

I cross the grounds, focusing solely on the warm sun, letting it burn away the cold remnants of his lust.

I do not slow down till I am sure his eyes no longer sear my back.

I pause, exhaling my vexation, as I lean on the rail of the bridge which arches over the small fish pond.

I stare at it intently. I am fairly certain *this* pond is not recorded anywhere in my mother's sketchbook.

My fingers grip the wood and I close my eyes, raising my face to the sun.

"Miss Teagarden?" My heart leaps at the deep rumble that is his voice

Brighton stands beside me; I feel and smell him. Our arms touch and mine prickles with pimpled gooseflesh.

I open my eyes and turn toward him, smiling. I think of Jonesy's warning words, but I am...*drawn* to him. Like a moth to his proverbial flame; so much so, I will endure the scorching.

He is smiling slightly at the use of my surname.

"I have been waiting to see you, but you have been...absent...of late."

"Why, Mr. LeFroy? What did you need me for? The second symphony? I know we need to work on it, it is just—"

He places a singular finger against my lips, quieting me. My eyes widen at this unexpected show of attention. He is always aloof, calculating.

His warm, calloused hand slides over mine and my heart vaults upward, lodging in my windpipe.

He turns my palm over and I resist the urge to close my eyes and savor every bit of his touch.

The feel of cold metal suddenly encircles my index digit, but in the space of a blink, turns curiously *warm* against my skin. The band is a simple silver design.

I cock my head, raising my hand to the sun to stare at it. "Whatever in the world is this?"

His lips press to a thin line. "It is what is loosely referred to as a *cramp ring*."

A flicker of memory as my mind recalls my governess, proper Miss Potts, and her scoffing derision over this very issue during a history lesson.

"From the 14th century? Was not their power to have been borne of a King's blessing upon a ring? Mr. LeFroy, you surprise me. I would not take you for a superstitious man?"

He slides the band around my finger in a circle and the heat intensifies and the throb in my finger...*quiets*. I blink repeatedly and I shiver.

"That is not possible." I flex my hand open and closed. Not a pinch of pain.

"The power was not from the King's blessing. That portion was indeed a wives' tale. There were a finite number of rings forged, with specific metallurgical properties—"

My eyebrows bunch and he amends, "Specific metals. Used for centuries in healing. Once known only to the Pharaohs."

"And *this*, is one such ring?" I stare at it with equal reverence and horror.

He nods gruffly. "Cannot have that precious cello-hand lame, now can we?"

My finger is noticeably less swollen. Mother was right about one fact, Charleston is special. Will the wonders of this place never cease?

"Where would one acquire such a ring?"

He ignores my question, his eyes scrutinizing my hair. "I see you used the Henna."

"Yes." I playfully turned my head right and left, wiggling my eyebrows, letting him admire my handiwork. "Better?"

He shakes his head. "No. I expect your true color is magnificent. I would very much like to see it someday." His finger boldly strays to the dark ringlet of my wig, to ease it behind my shoulder.

My breath catches and I remind myself to breathe.

"Perhaps. Perhaps we might trade secrets."

And you could tell me about those animals, about that island. About your Samson-like strength.

His eyes narrow and his expression turns as black as the storms he chases. He gives me a stiff tip of his hat. "Good day, Miss Teagarden."

Without thinking, I clutch his arm. "*Allegra*. Call me Allegra. And please don't go. I'm—I'm sorry. You can keep your secrets."

He pauses, turning back. His mouth tightens and his words slip out through gritted teeth, "I. Don't *want* to. I *have* to."

The sadness in his eyes cuts to my core. It is as deep and fathomless as the water's where we both search for answers.

He strides from the bridge into the cover of the giant Oak tree.

I follow, pleading, "Please, Brighton, don't go. Not yet."

He halts and spins back and leans in—so close and so quick, his breath caresses my cheek.

The slight tremor in his voice betrays his emotion. "I would love nothing better to confide my secrets. To unload this heavy burden that weighs down my very soul. But...that would be best *for me*. Not you. There is safety in ignorance, Allegra."

The cry of the animals fills my head. *Could he be capable of such cruelty?* But the rabbit stood up, in the end.

I stare at him. The stark tenderness in his voice; such sincerity could not be feigned. *Could it?*

He turns to leave, mistaking my far-away expression for a dismissal—but I slip my arm through his, securing it tightly. "Walk me to my rehearsal?"

He laughs nervously, staring at our linked arms, but his eyes concede. "Fine. No harm in that, I suppose."

We stroll past the white swans and the workers scuttling back and forth, repairing various rides.

"Where *have* you been, Mr. LeFroy? You swept in, sketched me pretty pictures, inspired a symphony, left me breathless with a chute ride and disappeared. Why, I felt like a common strumpet."

His face colors and he laughs loudly. His eyes dance as he regards me once again. "Oh, *you,* Miss Teagarden, are a truly dangerous creature."

"Dangerous enough to handle the likes of you."

My heart beats so fast I fight the swoon. I bite my lip.

Would he think me too bold? If I confess he *is* and *has been* in my every thought since I first laid eyes upon him?

I find the prospect of *not* telling him leaves a bigger hole than the gnawing fear of truth.

I leap. I hear the gravity in my own voice. I halt, forcing him to face me.

"Please, Brighton. Do not disappear again. I...merely wish to be in your presence. I care not if you confess anything, ever. Just. Stay with me? Allow me that?"

His mouth opens along with his eyes. He snaps it closed and licks his lips. "I. You deserve so much better than what I am able to offer, Allegra."

He continues his ardent stride and I struggle to keep pace with his long-legged steps.

I see the gazebo ahead and the occasional practice note floats to our ears.

My heart falls and I extricate my arm. "That is to be your excuse then, to let me down easy?"

The shake of his head is so fervent it sends his black curls falling across his forehead. "No, no, I assure you. But I'm afraid I find you much too interesting. Too consuming. I do not divide my obsessions well. I will never provide the life that all women wish for."

My eyebrows press down as I prickle with irritation. "You are presumptuous, sir, to assume to know the life which I desire. You know nothing of the sort. Of my desires."

He smiles. "Too true. Excuse my assumption. I scarcely know you." A storm wrinkles his brow, but he battles it, and the lines soon smooth.

"Come to the island tonight. I will prepare supper."

"Really?" I will my face calm, but my insides tremble.

He nods. "I'm quite positive this idea is dreadful, but seem to be unwilling to stop myself."

"I'm quite glad for your lack of self-control then."

"I shall come to collect you at dusk."

He shuffles backwards a few steps, his eyes holding me captive, and then swiftly turns back toward the Inn.

Jonesy registers my flushed face as I excuse my way down the row for rehearsal. I need not utter a word, he knows me well enough to guess.

"Are you *mad?*" His dark eyes regard me seriously. "Oh, laws. This will not end well."

Marietta, too, watches me. "Allegra. That man is evil. You must stay away from him."

"I cannot believe that," I whisper low enough for only Jonesy to hear. "I don't think I can."

CHAPTER NINE

Evening

"Blast. He shall arrive at any moment. Hurry
Jones. I should be fetching Allegra at this very
moment."

Jones glares, but says nothing.

I wrench back the threadbare curtains, trying in
vain to catch a glimpse of him through the thick
island foliage. *Nothing.* Just rain and green. So
much green.

My father seems to skip points in time—one
moment I am alone, the next, he is breathing down
my neck.

"Brighton, you detest him. Why do you permit
your father an audience?"

My eyes steal to the journals which litter the
table and I stare Jones down.

"You know perfectly well, why."

I stomp to the table and snatch up the leather-
bound evils, shoving them into his arms. A paper

slides out—one with hieroglyphics and an Egyptian eye I've yet to decipher. "Hide these. Now."

Jonesy's eyes cloud. His mouth pops open then shuts as he wrestles with the right words of chastisement.

I turn away. "I have no idea what protest is forming in that mind of yours, but he is *come*. Please!"

My face flushes with a surge of blood through my temples as I give the anger free reign; it has kept me breathing.

Through battles over slaves and state's rights and my father's egomaniacal need to own and control and subserviate his every desire.

Jones stalks out the door; finally taking my heed.

I *feel* it. A prickle on the back of my neck like someone watches. A craving; a beaten path to my very core—my body simultaneously worships and despises it.

I whirl, trying not to look at it.

Sweat dots my brow and my eyes dart, looking everywhere except the table. They tick, tick toward it, like time somehow lengthens.

A magnetic force calls to my soul from a supposedly inanimate substance.

My father's voice murmurs in my mind, "*The Elementi.*"

Its radiating heat is a pyre beneath my skin. I shiver as the air thrums with the palpable tension. Like the ghosts of Allegra's chords still whisper around the room.

My reluctant eyes come to rest on the tin of blanched powder.

A bitter taste dread fills my mouth; months and

116

months of work to activate it—to bring it to life.

But should I have resurrected it? Should I just move on, as Jonesy said?

I titrated, over and over, day after day. And still I am uncertain.

I pluck an empty vial from the shelf, carefully spooning the powder-mound inside.

The vial shakes as my fingers fumble and I grasp it tighter against my palm, closing my eyes.

They shoot back open and water, burning from the powder's proximity. The smell of sulfur and rotting eggs fills my nose.

With the tip of my finger, I lift a solitary snowflake of the crusty powder to eye-level. "You...should not exist."

My breath catches then pumps like a bellows. *Anger* and *pain* and *loss* crush my heart like a vice.

Why must my father insist on perfection? On conquering.

His land-lust is never satiated. He thinks nothing of trampling underfoot any and all innocents unfortunate enough to step in his path.

My finger edges closer, as if an invisible magnet has lodged in my mouth, intent on ingesting the powder.

My finger moves of its own accord. Moves to place the sparkling flake upon my tongue.

"Brighton!" Jonesy shouts.

My teeth snap shut, slicing through my bottom lip. I welcome the reorienting taste of blood as the tiny piece of destruction floats to the wooden floor.

The orange cat leaps from the sill and swallows it before landing.

"*What* are you doing? You are getting worse."

Jonesy strides to me, giving my shoulders a rough shake. "The grief—it's eating your mind. Making you daft. Perhaps. Perhaps it's time to let go…"

Rage refires, flushing my neck, burning up the sorrow. *"Forget?* What do you know of loss? Of failure? I failed. Failed to protect him."

Sorrow suffocates the fire under a wave of melancholy. My muscles seem infected by the despair and I collapse weakly into the chair.

Jonesy eases down too, his eyes careful. "George wouldn't want you to be miserable, Brighton. To stop living because of what happened to him."

My lips crack a feeble smile and one long streak of wetness escapes.

I shake my head, squeezing the bridge of my nose. "Of course not. But if there is *any chance* he lives. Anywhere. The *other place* we spoke of—"

"He is not your concern."

The room turns red. My hands ball to fists.

My father darkens the doorway, rain streaming from his hat.

I shoot up and hear the chair clatter behind and cross the space in seconds to strike his shoulder.

It jars backward, but his eyes never waver. Never blink. They glow softly; like the mother of pearl of a clam shell. If I do not stop, mine shall as well.

"He should be my concern. Not yours. You care only for *The Elementi.* Not for people. Not for love, for family. He was *like a child* you disgusting—"

"Temper, temper Brighton." His smile is sickening. "Your brother is beyond you now. You should return with me. Continue your research. You could do much good for the confederacy."

"I do not prescribe to your particular brand of

research? You do not wish to heal. You wish to *transcend*."

I rise to my full height, thrusting out my chest. We stare, eye to eye.

Jonesy hovers, his hands opening and closing, unsure when to strike.

My father's nostrils flare, his eyes narrow. "*You* have tasted the powder. I see it in your eyes. Why you almost glow." His smile spreads wider.

The shaking spreads from my hand to my entire person. "I am not like you. I know it to be an aberration. Knowledge we are not fit to possess."

"Humbug."

"Greed. And vanity. And power. That is what you seek." A bit of my spittle strikes his cheek.

He wipes it away without blinking. "Nay, that is what *I shall have*. With or without you. Once we succeed—things will change. We can be more than kings. We can be Gods."

Jonesy's breath intakes sharply. I know his thoughts. *Blasphemy.*

I nod. "Aye, you'll have it, no matter the casualties. I'll end up like George. The powder's a cheat. One must *battle* to use their life for good— reward without earning makes…someone like you." I thrust my finger toward the storm. "Do not return."

My father swaggers back toward the door, unflinching. "You will return home; *your people* draw you. They ask for you." He shrugs. "You need me to perfect the formula. You have seen him, haven't you? In your little pond. In the water."

I will my face calm. But I know he sees inside me, my motives. He sees *everything*, like some perverted, omniscient devil.

119

"Even if you found a reservoir. You know it will not open."

It shall.

"Go." I fling open the door. The wind catches it, banging it off the cottage. Torrents of rain stream from the porch roof like a waterfall garden.

My father steps from the porch, staring straight ahead. I slam the door and Jonesy throws the bolt behind him.

Jonesy's chest heaves. "Brighton. *Have* you seen him?"

I drop to the chair and cradle my head in my hands.

And nod.

CHAPTER TEN

Allegra

My behavior is highly improper. When *a gentleman* does not show for an engagement, *a lady* does not chase him down—let alone become a voyeur.

Yet, here I am, spying like a common criminal. Hunkered down in the grass beside his cottage. I might as well live on the isle for the amount of time I spending hiding on it.

I smile, basking in the horror it would cause my tight-laced, propriety-obsessed father.

When Brighton did not appear to collect me for our outing...no amount of Sarah's screaming and ranting could hold me in the bungalow.

The cats have returned, naturally. With my first footstep from boat to isle, they find me—purring and darting in and out of the surf in their hurry to get to me. I am some odd, feline magnet.

I stare down at the yellow winding about my legs

and shiver. "Apparently *you* don't agree with the lights. That I should stay away."

I dart through the ferns, heading directly for the cottage and grounds.

Fear is a heavy, tight ball in my stomach. But the desire to know Brighton's secrets overrides the anxiety; a constant ebb and flow of unanswered questions drowns my mind.

The front door opens and Brighton leaves the laboratory, walking briskly toward the shore.

My heart beats wild. *Will he discover my dingy on the north shore?*

I hold perfectly still, peek through the ferns, holding my breath.

He turns, heading south, away from the boat and my breath exhales in a *whoosh*. The world tilts as I wait for my heart to calm; hand over my mouth, as I fight to master the panic.

The cats wind and wind around my calves, under my skirt.

I wait until he is a speck on the horizon, and bolt toward the lab.

What are you looking for? Shouldn't you let him confess his secrets? When he trusts you?

"I...cannot."

It's the lights. And the horrible contradictions.

Brighton haunts my every thought and I dream...of staying with him.

I have never met a man such as him. I hate to be so bold, even in my thoughts, but when I am near, he seems to see naught but me. I have never known such kindness, such caring from a man. And despite the Sampson-like strength he possesses, his every touch laid upon my skin, is so very careful—as if I am a delicate vase. I swallow.

But *the lights, the cats, these abnormalities*— they ruin any possibility of a future with him.

"They bloody tell me to run."

I must know. I must banish all doubt before relinquishing the tiny, remaining bit of heart that hides from him.

I reach the lab and steal inside, my eyes sweeping. *The crooked man. Oh, my word, I forgot the crooked man. What if he is here inside?*

Fear screams at me to run. I bite down on my lip, forcing myself forward.

The old leather-bound journals lie face-open beside the Bunsen burners once again.

I close the last few steps and snatch one off the table. It's surprisingly dense and heavy and I huff as I flip the pages.

I try to think clearly—but panic buzzes; I shake my head, trying, trying to focus.

I dart back out the door, back into the brush, hugging the book against my chest.

I don't have long. He will return quickly I know.

I stand terrifyingly still—my mind whirling. *Where to go? Where to go?*

I bound down the path deciding on the pond. After a few minutes, my chest heaves and I slow to a walk.

I search left and right to assure I am truly alone.

I walk quickly for several minutes. The trees look familiar, and there is a well-worn passage through the foliage, but the water is nowhere. *I should've arrived by now.*

The pond is no more.

I stare up at the Magnolia trees, dripping with

Spanish moss and feel disoriented. "The pond was here. I know it."

The direction in my head tells me it's so—but there is *nothing*. More dirt. No silver lightning-poles.

Uncanny. The word pops in my head, alighting my neck with gooseflesh. I rub my arms, and check the woods. I am alone.

I slump to a log and crack open the book.

The handwriting in the book is pristine—nothing like Brighton's scratchings.

My eyebrows pull together.

Jump One: Electrons. Negative spinning. The powder has disappeared.

"I don't understand. What is..e-lectron?" I roll the word on my tongue like a foreign pill.

I turn the page and the beautiful handwriting degrades.

George. I only do this for George. His afflictions be many. The fits, the moanings—his intermittent mutism. I will persevere for him.

Jump Two: Pristine writing again; the words shaped like poetry.

I am changed. My rheumatism has fled. My joints are as supple as Brighton's. He has noticed. He is avoiding me. He suspects, I know. I do not know if he shall join me. He is very much his mother's son.

My eyes cast further down the parchment. I begin to flip through the journal, my fingers working as fast as my beating heart.

In the journal's center are pages and pages of letters and numbers and equations. My eyes whisk across the lines.

They mean nothing to me.

I suspect they mean everything to others.

To Brighton.

I carefully turn the pages, skimming for more of the scrawling. The author's desperation bleeds through his fingers onto the page.

I find one more, near the end.

Jump Five: He is gone. Lost to the storm, in a single, destructive strike. I administered too much.

Brighton is leaving, too; he cannot forgive me, no matter my intentions. He is short-sighted and a slave to his emotions, like his departed mother. His mind unable to grasp the larger implications for mankind.

"What is this?" My mind whirls like the wind around my head.

I stare up at the sky. It's darkening, the rain threatening again. I was lost in the pages. Too long. *Will Brighton have returned?*

I spring from the log and barrel down the path toward the cottage, not caring to be quiet. It's too late for quiet.

The cats bound ahead, their yellow and black ears disappearing beneath the blanket of green ferns.

Thunder crashes, so close my head and jaw vibrate. I reach the barn and hide behind it, clutching my chest.

The animal's *scrreech*—wailing like newborn babes.

They sense my presence. My eyes sting with tears. Litanies of howls whine and cry; begging for freedom. My back, leaning against the barn, hums with their agony.

I peek around the barn's side.

My eyes widen as my stomach leaps and plummets to puddle in my boots.

Two soldiers converse with Brighton. I recognize the red crest, spread-wide across their chest immediately.

They are come. They are come.

Images spiral like mental-smoke behind my eyes.

Me, locked in another opulent prison. My hand thrust into fat Lord Lumberton's. Never to run again. Never to leave my house unchaperoned.

The choking vice of domination suffocates, pressing down on my chest, thrusting its hand through my ribcage, intent on my heart.

My mind careens on and I press myself tighter against the barn's wall. I am panting. I must control it. They will hear me. I clap my hands over my mouth.

He will want children. Children—over whom I will have no say. Whom he might even take from me. To turn them against me. All in the name of an heir.

As father tried to do to momma and I. But I refused; refused to eat, refused to play, refused to be his little golden goose till he once again returned me to the safety of her arms.

My lips retracting in revulsion. Angry tears well

and drip from the tip of my nose, numerous as the raindrops as the desperation seeps in to set in my bones.

I think of mother. Of the water.

"Death is preferable."

I skulk around the other side, my hands feeling the knotty barn-wood, needing to hear the conversation.

"So, you have not seen the girl then?" The older officer demands.

"I have not seen any young woman who fits the description you've provided, no."

"Realize, sir, Lord Manners is determined to find his daughter."

"I assume you've considered all options? Perhaps she was kidnapped?" Brighton's voice is convincingly low and concerned.

The officer sighs. "There's been no ransom note."

"Well, I hope Lord Manners finds his daughter…what did you say her given name was?"

"Katherine."

"Katherine." He pauses. "I wish you safe journey back to England. This storm will squall, mark my words. I suggest you make your way to the mainland for your own safety."

"We will not be departing Charleston proper without Miss Manners. Alive or dead. Good evening Mr. LeFroy."

The soldiers cut back the short stone path then jog beneath the swaying, warning Magnolia's. Their gnarled arms whip back and forth in the rising tempest as if trying to prevent their escape.

Resignation arrives in a single moment, leaving me limp. I slide down the side of the barn and a bolt of pain shoots through my bottom as it connects with the wet ground. My head falls forward to my knees as my muscles give up. I bite down hard on my lip, but they tremble as a whimper escapes, and the animals join in, drowning my voice.

Searingly warm fingers wrap about my forearms, gently hauling me to stand.

My chest hitches as pain stabs between my shoulder blades. Futility weighs about my neck like a millstone. "He shall find me," I whisper and crumple in half, gripping my knees with my hands through my dress-folds, breathing hard.

"Oh, my dear." His voice murmurs close to my ear, thick with compassion.

My head tilts back and I am rising…cradled his arms. I bury my face in his chest, propriety long-forgotten, only to weep harder.

"Shh. Shh." His footfalls are rhythmic slapping sounds against the stones. They sound far off, as if I am dreaming.

"What if they return?"

I feel an arm muscle flex beneath my back and he chuckles ominously, "I hope they do."

I jam my eyes shut, wishing for a home, wishing for my mother.

He kicks the door open, ducking us inside. The heat hits instantly, the roar and crackle of the hearth pushing back the damp.

Something or someone shuffles across the room, but I keep my eyes tightly closed.

"Leave us, Bartholomew."

The crooked man. But the desire to see him is now like another's curiosity.

Pain. The pain is what is real. *My reality.* I'd managed to keep it at bay all these months, believing it behind me. That I was in control of my destiny.

He slides me into a bed. His bed. Warm, soft coverlets hold me tight as the smell of him wraps around me, wriggling into my heart, trying to take root.

"You are safe here. I will not let them take you. I will hide you, if need be."

I nod. Hot tears leak and trail to my neck.

The hot streaks of his fingertips, rough as crushed shells, brush them away.

My ridiculous hair slips. Brighton feels beneath the wig to find my clips and carefully removes it.

He releases my hair and I feel it tumble to my shoulders. His fingers rake through my curls, straightening; fanning them out with what seems a measured, practiced hand.

I shiver at his touch.

I open my eyes as my breath intakes. His face is inches from mine. Deep blue irises flecked with brown-gold, regard me. They blink as his lips part.

I lean forward, placing mine in the space between. He moans softly, but where his chest and legs graze mine, he goes rigid, resisting.

My hands grasp in the back of his hair and I press my lips harder, allowing my tongue to dart along his lips. He trembles, and I exhale as his arms slip to pull me flush.

His mouth opens as his warm tongue grazes

mine in a heated, seeking fervor and his hands slide to ball in my curls.

I feel the need in his kiss and his tongue; but his hands remain gentle, caressing my hair, my head, my cheeks. I quietly wonder how hands capable of snapping tree-trunks can manage so soft a touch.

I break the kiss, our eyes ticking back and forth searching the others.

My words fall out in a rush, "My father wants me to marry. A man thrice my age. Who cares nothing for me, wants to bed and breed me like a prized thoroughbred. My father...hates me."

He nods, listening, worrying his bottom lip.

"My father." My voice cracks. "Locked me away for days at a time. When my mother passed, any civility died in him. I was only a reminder of her. He's a cruel, cunning, sharp-witted man. Not to be trifled with."

Fear burns my chest. *I have not the right to involve him.* Brighton is wonderfully good, no matter other's opinions.

And I am dragging him into a nightmare. One that could potentially snuff out his life with one puff from my father's poison lips.

My eyes widen.

He seems to read my mind. "You are safe, Allegra." He smiles, his heavy-lidded eyes opening wider. "Or should I say, Katherine?"

My heart stops for a moment and I blurt, "Please do not call me that. My middle name is Allegra, given by my mother. And I've taken my mother's maiden name. Teagarden. *That* is my name. The other person, the trained-traveling-monkey, is dead to me."

"The name suits you. It feels good to know it; to no longer have you hiding from me. I have secrets, I, too, wish to confess." He swallows and I see a rare emotion cross his face. Fear.

"If I tell you, I shall not blame you for fleeing. But know, that my door...and truth be told, my heart, is always open to you. I have spent months trying and trying to avoid and ignore this..." his eyes cloud as he searches for the correct word. "This craving for you. I tried to put you from my mind, but found I could not continue with my goals. Unless I allowed myself to pursue you."

My heart soars, but guilt holds it down, like an anchor to the earth.

I leap, interrupting him. "I can scarcely believe it...I too, think of you every day. I refused to allow my heart to even hope for your love. But to allow this to *proceed*...is selfish on my part. You—" I stop as the pain thickens my throat. My eyes involuntarily flick to the books. "Obviously have your own worries. I should not compound them with mine."

His head whips to the journals and his eyes narrow. "I will not allow you to refuse. Our circumstances are both grim, I concede. I know this to be bold, but Allegra...will you be *happier*, if I do not...*court* you? Even if I wish to."

The contrast of such a tentative voice from so overpowering a man is near ridiculous and I almost giggle. But then a great appreciation swells. That I may be the object of his affection.

I press my lips together to smother the laugh, allowing hope to rise.

"I shall allow it. No matter how unreasonable. And it is wholly unreasonable."

"It is," he nods. His thin lips twist into a heart-wrenching grin. "This was not how I had planned our outing. Unforeseen circumstances arose. But I had dinner prepared. Do you think you can eat?"

I shrug.

"One moment." He disappears down a hallway, and I flop back into the warm blankets, listening to the howl of the wind battering the windows.

He returns, shaking me. I sit up blearily, confused. I must've drifted off again. "Come with me, Allegra."

He eases me out of bed, wrapping my arm through his. His chest, warm against my side, his legs, muscles bulging through his trousers, lights a fire.

Passion *explodes* in my heart; my mind and body like a pulsing, living embodiment of his fireworks. Running through me, bringing me to life. Risking my good name, my only recommendation.

I turn into him, grasping his shirt in both hands, pressing my lips to his.

His hesitation melts and his hands slide under me to cup my bottom. I gasp but hop onto his front, wrapping my legs around his waist.

He stumbles, roughly placing me to teeter onto a high chest of drawers.

He leaves my lips, kissing down my neck. "Allegra," he murmurs my name.

I stroke through his curls, savoring their texture.

Wondering at the impossibility of him, of us; but wanting nothing more than to stay right here, to keep our skin as one.

His eyes hold mine, his arched eyebrows severe.

His head tilts as his lips graze mine. Teasing,

gentle strokes. His eyes drift shut as his breath quickens.

Want rips open my chest, leaving my heart open and unprotected. And I fall, completely and fully.

I cringe inwardly. I've never felt anything so terrifyingly beautiful and dangerously consuming.

"Tell me. Tell me everything. Your secrets."

His eyes snap open, alive with the struggle. "I...don't think I should."

I touch his cheek and he leans into it, closing his eyes.

"*I've* confessed everything. It's dangerous to love me. To want me." My face flushes, realizing my presumption.

His eyes flick open. He notices my blush and grins. "I will decide what is dangerous. Not now, however. You must eat."

He slides me down, and taking my hand, leads me to small room encased by glass. A conservatory.

A myriad of plants crawl the walls. Red, full blooms adorn the vines like flowery fingers reaching for the sky and white magnolias smile down from an inside arbor, draped across the ceiling.

Small palmettos dot every corner, providing a contrast of green against the colored pinwheel of the flowers.

It is truly magnificent; as if the beauty of the woods was bred and raised in this very room.

I stare up, and imagine it on a sunny day.

Rain lambasts the room in angry sheets, sliding down the glass to distort the view of the surrounding forest.

Flickering candles huddle in every corner. A table set in silver offers a creamed soup and thick

crusty bread, and two glasses full of blood-red wine.
My face flushes deeper and a scratchy tickle fills
my throat. I clear it.

"For me?"

He nods, gesturing for me to sit. My hand fidgets
with my necklace as he pulls out the chair when it
becomes apparent I am rooted like the plants.

He takes his place across from me and ladles
soup into my bowl.

Brighton snaps open a napkin, and spreads it on
his lap. "We need to work on the new symphony.
Silas has been breathing down my neck."

I nod and take a small sip of the soup.

The constriction is immediate.

It tightens like a slip-knot, strangling.

My throat closes. My hands clutch at my neck. I
wheeze—my mouth gaping, sucking at the air like a
fish on dry dirt. My eyes seem to enlarge and bulge
with the increasing pressure in my chest.

I *hear* his chair clatter as my vision flickers.

"Allegra. Allegra! Whatever is wrong?"

Face flushing. Heat spreading. I see nothing, my
eyes open and blinking.

I point toward the soup and croak, "Oy-oyster."

"Merciful Father. Shellfish. You are allergic!
Barty!"

My knees crumple and a sharp pain like the
clanging of a bell as the back of my head strikes the
chair.

Brighton's hands catch my arms and ease me
down and I feel the cold stones against my neck.

Shuffling. "Sir?"

"Fetch the powder." His voice is stricken with
panic.

"No, sir. I shall not. You said—"

"Blast it, she will die! I don't care what I bloody-well-said. Do as I say, man!" Scrambling, beside my head. "I will do it myself."

Footsteps receding, returning.

My lips pry open. Drops, wetting my tongue, strangely acrid and hot.

Visions instantly erupt. Blinding-white-lights, the sound of my cello. The foreground of sound, of every piece I ever played, jumbled in a distortion of deep chords and jangling notes set in the background of my sighs, my weeping.

Blackness presses. The weight of a cannonball on my chest.

"Uh!" The unseen fist squeezing my lungs eases a fraction. I gasp and pant.

The air is coming but too slowly—like water down a constricted pipe. I am drowning on the cobblestones.

Brighton pulls me to his lap, rocking me. His whole body trembling. "Please. Please. Too much horror. Do not let her pass. I beg of you." Then quietly, as if to himself, "She is so very *good.* This time, take me."

The invisible hand issues a final clench in my chest and all is blackness.

I know not how long I have been gone, but it feels as if I am flying, suspended in air. But a bumpy ride, I am being jostled every which way. I force my eyes to open a slit.

I am cradled in Brighton's arms. He is running; the thick green of the forest rushes past on either side like a blurring whirlwind of jade.

My throat itches and burns as if scorpions jab

and jag the length of it from my mouth to my gut.

Free-falling. My stomach leaps. *How?*

Splaaaash. My head, beneath water. Warmth and wetness and pressure along the length of me. Like a massive, wondrously warm bath.

My face breaks the surface and his arms encircle me, floating me on my back, but keeping me close.

My chest slowly, slowly, slowly, begins to open—the invisible fist loosening its grip.

I gasp, my mouth open and working, beating back the flickering blackness. My ribs ache, fighting to expand against the dead-weight.

"That's it, my dove. *Breathe*, Allegra."

Lifting again, floating. Swirling.

The itching disappears. I swallow. My throat feels utterly normal. Better than normal.

I inhale deep soothing breaths, ignoring the light tap-tap-tap of the raindrops on my upturned face.

I open my eyes. Brighton floats me around a small pool, hidden beneath a canopy so thick the sky is almost entirely shut from view. A natural greenery tent of thorns and thistles.

His eyes are bright and terrified and his mouth a taut, hard line. I smile, trying to ease them.

"I'm alright." I stretch my legs, my fingers, my toes. "I am better than alright."

Any and all pain has fled my body. My finger is perfect, and I flex it against my palm in the water. A symphony *explodes* in my mind, my fingers twitch, automatically grasping at the notes. It is then I notice the smell. Sulpher.

And I see the pinpricks of light above the thistle canopy and had mistaken them for stars in my previous delirium.

My breath intakes as I realize the fireflies swarm over the thistle hut, their iridescent bodies sparkling like sunlight upon snow.

Brighton releases me and I try to find my footing as my head dips below the waterline. A bit of the bitter water leaks into my mouth.

It is continuously warm. How is that possible?

"There is no bottom, tread water and swim to the side. It's...very deep." There is something ominous in his voice. He looks angry.

"Brighton. I feel." I search for the precise word. "Marvelous. Like I've never felt before."

He sighs heavily, then the words pour out so fast I strain to catch them. "Yes. I had no choice. You stopped breathing. And I just. I just couldn't let you go. Not yet. Not when I must get to know you Allegra. I may be no better than my father to intervene in your passing." He shakes his head. "No. I'm through with half-truths. I must *have you*, Allegra."

My heart expands in my chest, next to bursting. But a seed of fear burns at its beating center. "Brighton. Nothing would make me happier. But, what is this pool? I have so many questions. And I need the answers."

My mind flutters to my mother's sketchbook. Had she seen this pool as well?

We have reached the side of the pool and we clutch its stony sides, our feet treading below, hidden in the murky water.

His voice is so grave, gooseflesh rises on my skin. "I only wish to protect you. My secrets are dangerous. If I tell you, you too, will be at risk. That is why I resisted you; I never wanted to bring you into…" His eyes sweep the pool, the fireflies. "All of this. I will tell you a piece at a time, keeping you as safe as I can. Can you accept that proposal?"

"I suppose so."

"These pools are the reason I am on the isle. No one knows of them. It is vital you not reveal their location. You may find you've developed…new traits from bathing in its water."

A tingle of fear slithers up my spine. "How so?"

"It is different for everyone. Come to me with whatever it is, and I shall try to explain."

He smiles widely. "Your hair. The water removed all traces of the Henna, and your eyebrows as well." His voice is gruff. "It's lovely to see you, as you—Allegra Teagarden. Your hair is the loveliest shade of strawberry-blonde."

I smile in return but it falters. "My fingers are beginning to tingle."

"Ah. We need to get out of the water."

CHAPTER ELEVEN

Burning. I feel as if I am on fire.

Heat begins in the small of my back and radiates up, tendrils extending over my arms, legs, belly and breasts, culminating in a searing cluster of pain—like a branding iron, on my chest.

I sit up too quickly and stars pop in my vision as I reach for the bedside water-pitcher, awkwardly spilling half down my shift. To douse the pyre between my breasts.

My teeth chatter violently—*the world is changed*. Something is off. Or wrong.

The moonlight shines through the window and outside the fireflies bob around my window like tiny lighted sentries.

Same guest room in Brighton's cottage. My meager belongings at the foot of the bed.

I force my eyes closed and breathe deeply, feeling my nostrils flare.

I analyze my body, flexing and bending each part; the only pain is from the heat. I open my eyes and blink—my vision is unchanged.

A *blast* of music, an internal orchestra, *vibrates* the inside of my head, knocking me sideways with the force and I collapse to the bed, panting.

I had music in my mind every day, long before I could speak.

But it was always the cello which carried the melodies. It sang naturally to me, filling my days, lulling me to sleep at night.

To imagine the melodies of the other instruments was work. At times, it took months.

But now...

I force myself to listen. Listen to the inner workings of my mind.

Every instrument *sings*, in concert—violins, percussion, horns and chimes all meld and blend in a musical weaving of melody and harmony.

I slide from the bed and pace, frantic to find paper. To put it to paper before it leaves me. I think of Heir Mozart.

I have read everything about the man I could find. It was the only time my father ever honored a request, assisting me to every journal and paper he came across on the prodigy, assuming it would translate into coin for him.

Mozart began to play at three. I was closer to nine. I was gifted, but not a prodigy. But now...

I sway and twirl in a circle on my tip-toes, my arms raised to the heavens, astounded and awed by the sounds between my ears.

I whirl as a scuttling sound blasts the side of my head and cover my ears, crouching down, panting against its force.

My eyes tick across the floor. A mouse.

But how? A mouse could not make such a terrible, ear-crushing racket.

I must find parchment. Brighton's supply is exhausted, he has told me so just last eve.

I fling open my door and hurry across the darkness of the parlor and out the front door. A tiny voice beneath the orchestra screams, *impulsive,* but this compulsion to rid my mind of the music drives me forward.

The travel through the isle's ferns to the water and across the bay seems a dream, and I awaken to find myself hurrying down the Fancy's thoroughfare…toward the white, flapping tent.

It almost seems illuminated, like a ghostly specter in the inky Charleston night.

My heart flutters uncontrollably.

Sounds are deafening. Crushing. I wince, again and again—I hear too much.

The cicada's call, the cry of gulls, the crunch of the stones beneath my boots…my eyes quickly flick to the Spanish moss dangling from the oaks. I swear I *hear a spider*, crawling through its mossy tendrils.

That. Is not possible.

But is it? Anything and all seems possible with The Elementi.

I struggle, erecting a barrier inside against them, against the pain.

They dampen slightly and I smile.

I reach the tent and sigh. It is almost dawn. Light's pink fingers are showing at the horizon as if a giant, grasping the rim of the earth.

Silas insisted the instruments be left here in the tent, safely tucked in their cases for today's rehearsal.

Or to assure their owner's would not be escaping this night, as rumors of war intensify.

I drop to my knees and click open the case. A violin rests inside.

I instantly *see* and *hear* and *feel* the notes of the symphony dance behind my eyes and across my skin like a million tiny musical breaths, waiting to be born.

My fingers twitch to touch the neck. *I know how to play it.*

My eyes skip over the cases, one by one, and my fingers twitch out the notes, each instrument, each note, like a breath released.

I smile, but my lips tremble in a terrified quiver. I can play them all. Now.

I lift out the violin, slip it beneath my chin...and the dance begins.

The remaining night passes in a haze; my fingers upon every string, every neck, pounding out each beat like a musical debauchery.

Hours later, my fingers and shoulders sore and screaming, I collapse in the tent's center. My white dress tangled across my stretched, empty form.

I feel warmth as I am cradled against a chest. I snuggle closer with the familiar smell as Brighton takes me away, back into the night.

Back to the isle.

Three days later

Silas turns to face Plimpton, giving him a rare audience. The conductor squirms under his scrutinizing gaze.

"So you are telling me, Plimpton, Miss Teagarden reads the score once, and plays it from memory?"

"Yes, sir. She can play *all* the parts, from one look. She plays every instrument."

"Balderdash," Jonesy says. His face is still and smooth but I recognize the terror in his eyes.

"Jones, have you ever seen such ability? You are close with Miss Teagarden?" I add, trying to dissuade the greedy glint in Silas's gaze.

"She is a gifted cellist, yes. But this ability you claim..." Jones hedges.

"I have witnessed it with my own eyes!" Plimpton is red-faced and sweating as he blots it with his handkerchief, his own piggy-terrified-eyes never leaving Silas.

"Calm yourself, Jakob. I believe you. But I shall have to see for myself. This makes Miss Teagarden even more valuable. Indispensable, even." Silas paces, rubbing his hands, undoubtedly seeing the coins spin out from her cello as was Rumplestiltskin's spun gold.

Jones and I exchange a significant glance. A single muscle twitches beneath his eye.

"Bring her to me," Silas commands.

"She is ill," Jonesy spits, too fast.

Silas's eyebrows disappear beneath his blue-black hair. "Well, then I shall fetch a physician. I must see this for myself." He turns to me. "LeFroy, is your new symphony and accompanying celestial star-show complete?"

I thrust the papers into his hand.

His eyes scan the music, and he flips it to Plimpton. "Copy this, and distribute it—it's your new production. One week."

Plimpton dabs his head once again, his mutton sideburns quivering. "Yes, sir." He lumbers from the study.

"I shall send for the doctor," Silas says, turning to leave the room.

Jones and I follow without needing a word. This is all my doing. My gut clenches with guilt and a fierce protective surge lights in my chest.

I must get Allegra away from here. This instant.

I am dreaming. Of sharkskin. The leviathan swims past me, rubbing against my wrists. I am drowning in a swirl of white magnolias descending to the sea bottom. My heart goes apoplectic and then surges crazily.

My eyes flutter open as my heart has scrambled up my throat to beat in my mouth. *Where am I?*

I blink, befuddled, trying to recall the past day's events.

Brighton insisted I stay here on the isle, to monitor any new abilities that might transpire after my bath with the Elementi. So that he might offer counsel, having been through it himself.

Sarah is aghast, but I vowed her to silence. It has been risky, getting back to the isle after orchestra practice without being noticed by Silas. It is Sunday. No practice today.

Rough scratching on my wrists. I blink and blink, trying to clear the bleary film which seems to coat my eyes and finally manage to wrench them wide.

It was not sharkskin in my dream. The orange tabby cat—its scaly tongue licks the inside of my wrist. The feline *glows* in the dim room. And it is naught from the moonlight. It is brighter, more vibrant; as if the morning sun shines upon its fur. My breath intakes. I hold my arm aloft, flexing my fingers before my face.

A slight glow erupts and twinkles upon my normally-sallow skin. Like Mother-of-Pearl.

"What am I?"

The Elementi heals, improves…but is mankind meant to possess it?

I take in deep breaths, trying to calm myself.

I stare out the window. More rain, more lightning.

The fireflies flit into my room through a slit in the window-sill and quickly wrap around both wrists. I freeze, holding both hands up, slowly rotating them back and forth in disbelief. They blink on and off in a pattern. Communicating once again.

Brighton said, anything that ingested the element would be changed, its normal abilities enhanced. My eyes flick between the tabby and the fireflies. A prickle of unease sets in my chest. These creatures mean me no harm, and they warned me. Warned me to stay away.

I must relearn Morse code.

I ease back down into my coverlets, placing my arms crossed on my chest, afraid of hurting them and equally afraid of *why* they are about my wrists.

145

Waves of panic shudder through my limbs. My breath hitches hard as I squeeze my eyes closed, fighting the panic.

I hear a door open and my muscles go rigid. "Who's. Who is there?" My eyes fly open.

The footsteps falter behind the door. It creaks open to reveal the crooked man. *Barty,* is the name Brighton had called him.

The whites of his eyes, contrasted against his black skin make him more daunting, more dream-like.

I flip my legs to the bed's edge and shake my hands—resulting in a blinding white exodus from my wrists as the fireflies disperse.

"Please don't get up, mam. You might hurt yourself. Master Brighton says you are not yet well."

His speech is perfect. My eyes trail over him; his spine is bent, his right leg drags. His neck crooked to one side as if in a permanent shrug. But *something* is different from my first glance, weeks ago through the windows.

I swallow. "I am Allegra."

He smiles and all apprehension leaks from my muscles, leaving me weak.

"I know who you are. I am Bartholomew."

"Are you Mr. LeFroy's servant?"

His eyebrows knit tight. "No, mam. Mr. LeFroy, does not believe in servants. I earn my wages and stay of my own accord. *Somebody* has to look after the crazy fool."

My mind whirls through recent headline: Harper's Bazaar has run articles about Abraham Lincoln and his views of slavery. In the back rooms

146

of Charleston, one word is whispered: *secession.*
The battle over humans. It sickens me. If *I* am ever
free, I will fight so they shall be also.

Brighton appears behind him and claps
Bartholomew on the back. His face is taut and
guarded, as if he fights an underlying worry.

"Bartholomew, I need a word with Miss
Allegra—but don't go far—I need to speak to you
as well."

"You are an abolitionist."

His face is placid, evaluating my reaction. "Yes,
its blasphemy here. Don't say it too loud or I may
find myself strung from a tree."

The fireflies flit about the room, and he ignores
them.

I huff, and stare directly at the swarm, hovering
near the window.

He opens the armoire to extract a steamer trunk
and begins whipping clothes pell-mell inside it.

"Going somewhere?" My face grows hotter with
every flung garment. Could he be leaving me?
Sweep me off my feet, save my life and leave me?

"Yes, and so are you."

"Brighton—I cannot leave—I—"

He turns to stare, his face rigid. "Your *father's
soldiers* are sniffing everywhere. Literally. I saw
them with dogs today in Charleston. And now, Silas
has learned you have a particular talent for
memorizing music—is it true?"

"Why, yes. I always could. But now—one
glimpse and it all appears in my mind. And every
instrument. However did he know?"

"Plimpton must have been watching you the
other night in the tent, and now he's told Silas. He

has deemed you indispensable. Which means he will do anything, *anything* to keep you here." His face is taut and his mouth pulled in a grimace.

"Silas is very dangerous. I fear for your safety." He bends to pick up black boots. "And your chastity."

I stand and my head swoons. I collapse back down.

He sighs. "Blasted element. We must go. Barty!"

The dingy rises and falls on the white wave tips, cutting toward the mainland. I keep my eyes on the horizon, my queasiness still present and accounted for in my belly.

Nausea. My mother was very ill with me when pregnant. A longing stirs; I shall never have a child. Not while I am under the constant threat of my father's yoke.

A yearning tickles as I regard Brighton's broad shoulders, his beautiful black curls. I wish. I would wish for a child with him.

Brighton stares up at the lightning and his lips move, driving away my never-possibles.

"Are you counting the flashes?"

His eyes stay steadfastly fixed upon the sky. "Yes. And how quickly the thunder arrives after the flash."

My anxiety and hope burn a hole in my chest and I blurt, "I have so many questions. The cats, the fireflies—why do they cling to me now?"

His eyes tighten. "I will explain, Allegra. I owe you that, but there isn't time now."

"And. And those books?" My guilt seizes my tongue and the words spill out. "I'm so sorry. I took the books. I read them. I don't understand half of what I read—but it seems bad. Like a sort of black magic."

He laughs bitterly and his voice rises, his eyes violent. "It is *science*. Not magic. However to some, it might seem to be one and the same." His eyes cast to the heavens. "Its *origin* may be celestial, however."

We reach the dock and mercifully, no one is there.

"I must return to my bungalow. Please?"

"What? Out of the question! Silas was fetching a physician; it will only be hours till they discover you are missing."

"Sarah shall be frantic. My cello, I can't leave it. Sarah isn't like me—she'll be terrified alone."

"I will send word to Jones. Perhaps this will accelerate his plans."

He grabs my arm, hauling me up the path that winds along the water toward the dock-proper. His grasp is iron in his fear. "Ow!"

He quickly releases me as fear dawns on his face. "I am so sorry, my darling. When I am...distressed, I forget myself and the strength."

He gently grasps my other hand but continues at the break-neck pace.

"What plans?" I prompt him. Then comprehension dawns. "He is going to ask Sarah for her hand?" Tears fill my eyes.

How utterly wonderful. My lady's maid—her own lady.

"Yes, Jones shall not let any harm come to Sarah."

I nod, slightly relieved and look up to see white

sails billowing against the hard wind. "Where are we going—?"

"Mister LeFroy!" A huge black man bellows down from the schooner, grinning like a school-boy. "Oh laws it is *so good* to see your face! Let me look at you!" Brighton's returning smile is bright as his fireworks. "Toby! I am so pleased you came!"

A brigade of black men, young and old, crowd the deck, struggling for a glance to see us. "Who is *this?*"

I blush furiously.

Brighton takes my hand, helping me traverse the gang-plank. "*This* is Miss Allegra Teagarden. And we need to hide her."

Toby shakes his head. "Oh, sir. What have you gone and done now?"

Brighton helps me step down, eyeing the big many wryly. "Nothing you wouldn't do."

He gives a mischievous grin. "I reckon."

"Hurry. Allegra, come away from the rail."

Men come to clap him on the back, one by one, till he's grasped every hand, embraced every set of open arms. And his smile. Never did I see *that smile* all the while he was in Charleston's Fancy.

This was someone else entirely. *As if he were home.*

I think of his cottage. The most expensive items in it were the science pieces.

The telescopes, the Bunsen Burners, the microscope.

Otherwise he lived like a pauper; a slave, like me, to Silas.

"How on earth did you afford to charter this schooner?"

He turns, evaluating my face.

"Not that I don't appreciate it," I prompt.

Toby stares, his dark eyes confused. "Miss. This is *Mr. LeFroy's* schooner."

"Technically—it's my fathers. We never finished the transference papers."

The man's eyes roll. "Your father. Things have been dreadful-awful with you gone. He ain't never there—your step-mother, she just crazy—and your brother—"

"Hides in Charleston at his office."

Toby nods. "Did you find what you came for?"

"Yes. And no. I haven't finished yet."

Toby shakes his head and turns back to the bow. I'm speechless. "You...aren't poor?"

"No, but it is highly reassuring you would take me with nothing." He smiles. "Will you think less of me?"

I laugh out loud. "Why on earth are you holed up on a floating rock, under the boot heel of such a slimy man?"

"Silas owns the isle. It has something I need."

"Related to the books. Related to the Elementi?"

"Yes."

The ponds. It is something with the ponds.

Brighton heads to the front of the ship until Charleston is no longer visible on the horizon. I busy myself, staring out at the waves. At the birds bobbing on the waves and the occasional dolphin beneath the surface.

He sits by me once again, gathering both my hands in his. I can't help but notice the shocked expression on several of the men's faces.

Brighton's lips press together and his nostrils flare. "I need you to listen very carefully."

I nod and wait, unmoving.

"My father...is a pitcher plant." His eyes are pinched, as if the words are painful. "Do you know what that is?'

I smile, trying to assuage that look.

"Do not laugh, Allegra. This is not a game. A pitcher plant attracts pretty bugs, *like you*. Perhaps by pretty gowns or lovely meals, to dull your senses. Then, once inside, the sides of the plant are slippery, inescapable. The pretty bug is trapped. Then drowned, then eaten." His entire body shakes and his hands grip mine so tightly, pain shoots through my now-perfect fingers. "He will *eat you*, do you understand?"

My shoulders shake. He notices, and rubs them, but his expression doesn't soften. "Good. Be afraid. Be very afraid. It may save you."

I shake my head. "You are so learned...I don't understand. How does your father make his fortune?"

"Rice. My father deals in rice." He turns to stare at Toby. "And humans. He buys and sells humans."

CHAPTER TWELVE

"Why did we come by schooner, instead of carriage?"

Several sets of black eyes flick across my face in question, smile and then quickly dart away.

Toby, however, guffaws. "She ain' been round the Carolina's long, has she?"

Another slip. I sigh self-consciously.

Brighton, however, does not laugh. "To travel by road would take days, by water, only hours."

His hand strays to his pocket, extracting a crumpled piece of parchment. "I found this posted in Charleston, several weeks ago."

My hands fly to my mouth as I stare down at the rendering...of me.

I am depicted by my true hair color and the artist has certainly captured my face. A ripple of fear courses down my arms and my teeth worry my bottom lip.

Beneath the very-well-drawn likeness are the words, 'Missing, Katherine Manners-Reward'.

Brighton's warm hand grips my shoulder and

squeezes. "I am certain the soldiers scour the main highways, searching for you. And now any other gold-digger in the South."

I nod and swallow. I have no words. Father will stop at nothing to find me—and it's only for spite. To think he actually pines for me is ludicrous.

Gooseflesh erupts as his scowling face invades my thoughts. I rub my hands together to ward off the image.

Brighton takes my hand, leading me to a pile of blankets. "Sleep. You will need your strength tomorrow. I'm afraid our stay will be no respite. My family is…"

He stares up at the white sails, flapping in the night air like the ghosts of our past.

I touch his arm. "There is nothing your family can do that I haven't witnessed in my own. Fortune and privilege, which should mean decency and honor, often breed the exact opposite sort of men."

A strange sound rips through the night—like the wind has somehow solidified and is now being chopped through a waterwheel. The hair on my arms rises to cover the gooseflesh.

"*What* was that?"

He hesitates, "*That* is an alligator."

I sit straight up, craning to see the leviathan from over the boat's edge.

"He's behind us now, probably already below water. Yet another reason to travel the waters with a knowledgeable guide."

The smell of smoke wafts across the deck and I automatically cover my mouth. Brighton's eyes widen and he stands, squinting into the night.

154

Footsteps stampede from every direction of the deck to stare over the side that faces the shore.

I follow behind to the rail, leaning left and right, trying to see around the cluster of men.

Bright orange flames lick the inky sky from the shore. A high clock tower and steeple proudly juts out of the flickering center.

"It's a church," I whisper. "Was it arson?"

Brighton's eyebrows pull tight, becoming one. "Fires are a grim reality here. Even with kitchens detached from the main houses. It's the reason we now have twelve bloody fire brigades."

His brow furrow deepens.

Toby grunts and says softly, "I hope there weren't no people in that church."

"It's night?" I say, confused.

Toby and Brighton exchange a dark look. "Charleston is more dangerous every day. All this talk of the southern state's succeeding from the Union. Many men meet in secret; plotting and whispering our nation to war."

"They are serious? How would they defend against larger countries? Why do they wish to succeed?"

Brighton detaches me from the rail, leading me back to the blankets. I lie down, my head spinning. I feel certain I shall never sleep now.

He kneels; plumping a pillow beneath my head. His fingers linger in my hair and I sigh, a rare feeling of comfort flowing through me.

"I will tell you all you wish to know. Forewarned is forearmed. But for now, sleep. I will wake you soon."

I close my eyes to placate him...and hear not another sound.

The burning against my cheek rouses me from a too-heavy slumber. I sit up, blinking, shielding my eyes. "So much for waking me." The sun streams across the deck and the heat is already stifling.

Everywhere, men scurry around me and I wonder how I ever managed to sleep amidst such bustling.

Brighton stands at the helm, his white shirt and dark hair blow in the warm morning breeze. I stand; my legs sore and stiff and walk tentatively toward him. His knuckles are white and his tendons beneath stand out as he grips the railing.

I slide beside him and he startles but instantly calms at my presence.

He flashes me a wide, wry smile and nods forward. "That, be Morelands Estate."

I turn slowly and fight to stop the intake of my breath as I behold his home.

The estate proper is fixed directly off the river and a long, winding stone fence with spiraling, wrought-iron gates encase a tall manor of dark brick. Tall, round windows tower on either side, staring down at us, even from this distance.

The house reminds me of an overpowering grandfather—filling me with equal parts awe and trepidation.

Brighton points. "Rice fields." Already, throngs of black men and women wade into the waters to begin their day.

"There are so many…slaves."

Brighton bites the side of his mouth then purses

his lips, nodding slowly. He inhales slowly as if to control the words, "To keep a rice field running, it takes a great number of slaves."

"My word." I turned to stare at them, astounded by their sheer number. His fortune must be vast.

"H-How large is Moreland?" I clear my throat to hide my choke.

Brighton turns to stare, carefully evaluating my expression. I have never told him of my stand on slavery.

"My father owns six estates, spanning the entire length of the eastern seaboard. Pennsylvania, Maine...he believes in diversification for safety. By far, Moreland is the most taxing to run due to the sheer manpower needed. It is also by far the most lucrative."

The ship docks and the world and following moments turn hypnagogic; Brighton's taking my arm, leading me up the rambling stone path to the gate—all like a walk through a dream.

"Brrrighton!" A shrill voice like a warbling loon dissolves the fantasy.

A young woman, clad in blinding, pristine white, barrels out the estate front door; her dark hair flying behind her like a black, whipping flag; the color identical to Brighton's.

Brighton begins to laugh, low and joyous beside me, shaking his head.

"Oh, my good merciful word, you've finally returned!" the girl calls.

She trips, stumbles and rights all in a breath, wrenching her long white skirt aloft to expose bare ankles. "I am *so* vexed. You were gone far, far too long."

Sheep scatter like a wooly-white-sea to dart out of her way. Geese squawk in chastisement, erupting in a white burst of wings to the sky.

A dog yips, biting at her heels in hot pursuit, whipped into a frenzy by her sprint. It zags in and out, just missing her legs.

I cringe and squint in anticipation—picturing another tumble.

She dodges, spins, and continues her bolt. The woman-child slides to a stop, spraying us both in a shower of rock, her ample chest now heaving.

She thrusts out her hand to pump mine, completely, utterly inappropriately. I giggle. I cannot help it.

"Lucy. I'm Lucy. Who the Tom Fool are you?"

Brighton bursts out laughing. He bends in half, his hands on his knees as he tries to regain control. "Oh, *Lucy*. How I have missed you."

He clears his throat, wipes his eyes and waves his hands with a flourish. "Allegra, this is my sister, Lucy. Lucille Elizabeth Annabelle Moreland. This is Miss Allegra Teagarden."

She rolls her eyes, "Just Lucy."

I stare, doing a quick assessment. I estimate her age to be about fifteen by her girlish buoyance and blossoming figure.

Lucy's eyes narrow. "Is she your particular friend?"

My cheeks instantly blaze but Brighton guffaws again. "Oh, my dear, you must learn to keep that tongue in check. I see that has not changed a wit."

Brighton takes our arms, one on either side of him, steeling us toward the grandfather-house.

My eyes drop under its unnerving stare.

"*Well, is she*? You didn't answer my question? That has not changed, either," she nearly growls.

Brighton gives her a sidelong glance. "Yes. She is."

Lucy stops dead. Brighton relinquishes her arm and keeps walking.

I crane my neck back to see the look on her face.

"I *do not* believe it. I never, ever thought I would see it."

She dashes to catch up, lacing her arm through mine this time. "Miss Allegra Teagarden. You are a truly remarkable creature, because I never, ever thought I'd see the day my brother would utter those words—he—"

"Enough, darling. Where is Papa?"

Lucy's demeanor instantly shifts, like the wind leaving the sails. "He has been gone for a week, to New York, I believe. And you know Danvers, he's so tiresome. It's been dreadful-lonesome without you...and without George."

Brighton's eyes tighten and he swallows. "Yes, I'm sure it has been my dove. It's just too dangerous to have you with me. You are safe at Moreland. One day, I will be finished with my research, and your life will change again."

Lucy's chin quivers. "Do you promise, Brighton? Promise this time you won't stay away so long. It's dreadful here without you."

I feel a lump rise in my throat. My own loneliness reflects from the young girl's eyes. Lucy's desperation resurrects my own—one of the most ardent reasons for my flight.

"I know I am irreplaceable," he jests, trying to restore her mood. "But surely Annie and Toby and

159

Abigail have been keeping you busy." His smile is warm and almost fatherly. He is at least ten years her senior. I am much closer in age to her than he.

Her shoulders lift in an indifferent shrug.

A tall young man stands in the open doorway. "Master Moreland. There has been word from your father. I need to speak with you."

Brighton meets my gaze and speaks low, "Do not leave this plantation unless I have said so. Do you understand?"

I nod and swallow.

"Lucy, my darling. Might you show *my particular friend* about?"

Both Lucy and her black ringlets bounce. "Of course."

"I will see you this evening."

"What do you mean she is *gone?*" Silas's eyes are black fire. He rounds on Sarah and I instinctively step in front of her. My eye line is flush with the man's nipples—but I shall rip them off if the need be.

"She just d-didn't come back." Sarah's face crumples and she hides it in her hands.

I'm very glad now I didn't tell her of Brighton's note. Sarah is like a willowy flower; delicate and easily trampled. No doubt she would've unwittingly revealed her friend's whereabouts.

Silas glares at me. "*You.* Where is she? And Brighton?" A vein pulses in his forehead. He begins striding back and forth across Sarah's tiny sitting room.

"I know—you are clever. I know—you are loyal. And I know—you will lie for them." He halts, whirling. "I also know—*You* need *me*. And Charleston's Fancy. Where are they Jones?"

I thrust back my shoulders and my hands clench of their own accord. At the ready for the opportunity to pummel Silas's pointy-face.

"I do not know." My voice is even and true.

He lunges, his lips retracted like a jackal. I spin from his grasp.

Sarah chokes out a cry and scuttles out of the way.

His fist cocks, swinging madly. The uppercut hums past my ear, leaving his middle exposed. My fist connects with his gut in a one-two punch.

"*Oof.*"

His chest heaves and his eyebrows are high. "A musician who brawls. Seems there is more to you than I expected, Jones."

My father knew I would be small in stature. He paid dearly, coin he could ill-afford to have me trained…to defend myself against the ignorant ruffians of the world.

Silas was a ruffian, but not stupid. Indeed, Silas was brilliant. But what made him the most dangerous, was his capacity for cruelty. It seemed to envelope him like a cloak, leaving him impervious to any and all empathy.

I'd seen him *beat* the livestock before they were slaughtered, for sport—a maniacal grin on his rotten face. And his slaves when the spirit moved him.

Silas lunges for Sarah, wrapping her long red

hair in a tight fist. He tugs it and she whimpers, dropping to her knees before him.

"Let. Her. Go!" I bellow.

The words slip through his gritted teeth and emerge razor-sharp, "When you find out *where they are*—remember this *Percival* Jones. Allegra is *mine* to do as I please. I pay her way; she has no family, no means. She belongs *to me*. As do you."

My nostrils flare. I cannot leave. Not yet. "Release her."

His fingers relent and Sarah sobs.

I shall buy a pistol, and never be without it, till I can get Sarah away from this madman.

"You tell your friend Brighton I want my two most precious commodities returned post-haste. I, in turn, will not tell the soldiers who keep sniffing around Charleston that I know the location of their precious cargo."

I stride past him, easing Sarah from the floor and into my arms.

"If I cannot derive coin from the two of them, then the reward on her head shall be compensation enough, I suppose."

I hold perfectly still as he makes for the door. "Tell that fat choirboy Plimpton to ready Allegra's symphony. We shall perform it by Friday and I'll find some other firebug to do Brighton's job. How hard can it be?"

CHAPTER THIRTEEN

Jonesy

"Was that supposed to happen?" The lady beside me breathes. The white feathers of her swan costume ruffle as she clutches her husband's forearm.

The second masquerade, sans LeFroy *or* Allegra, has so far managed to be adequate. *No longer.*

Sarah's black eyes turn to meet my gaze as her hands clutch the boat's railing. A crash thunders overhead.

Her eyes widen in fear as the fireworks rain down, casting a blood-red glow across her upturned face.

Beside me, the orchestra struggles. Musician's shift with anxiety in their seats as they attempt to ignore the fire in the sky.

A muscle beneath Plimpton's eye flinches with every botched note like a muscular metronome.

We hadn't enough time to practice it. Allegra's

163

symphony was layered and marvelous—not a piece to be taken lightly.

Fear hums through the musician's rows; an unwanted harmony to the symphony's melody.

Ill-timed fireworks *collide* in fits and starts and pops, *too close* to our heads. Patrons' murmur, their voices unsure and nervous.

Silas glares at the light-show like a man possessed. A strange flashing light seems to emanate from him. I squint and swallow, realizing his time-piece reflects the light from his quivering hands. His lips draw back in a tight grimace I've come to associate with impending violence.

Brighton's replacement is aiming the pyrotechnics hair-singeingly close to his paying-patrons-heads.

Hoisting a megaphone, Silas bellows, "Isn't our lightshow wondrous? We shall be retiring inside now for refreshments—"

A hum hits our ears; grows louder and louder as the night becomes brighter.

A stray streak of blue light shoots toward Silas like a calculated cannonball. The rocket *slams* into the deck, smoldering then crackling to life.

Silas leaps away from the blaze as the megaphone clatters. The orchestra halts in a din of clangs and warbles.

Above, *two, four, six* pairs of rockets collide in mid-air. Instead of beautiful falling sparks, globs of burning fire rain down like dragon's breath.

They are too close. I shake my head. "Too close."

I spring from my orchestra chair and hurry through a litany of screams to the spot where Sarah stood, seconds before the crowd blocked her from my view.

Brighton had expertly calculated the angle and trajectory of the fire so it would harmlessly fall into the bay. But now—with the idiot randomly exploding rockets—I duck as a bolt of fire whisks past so close I feel the heat on my cheek.

Shrieks and shouts erupt as I weave and spin, trying to make my way to Sarah.

"Sarah!"

The fire is spreading across the riverboat's deck. I feel the heat at my back.

"Sarah!" I scream, the blaze incinerating my self-control.

"I'm here, Percy!"

I burst out of the thick crowd and sigh in relief and grasp her shaking hand to my chest.

Men and women retreat, scurrying backward across the deck in a jumbled mass of screams, away from the now-raging bonfire.

The musicians scatter, abandoning their chairs.

"Assemble the bucket brigade," Silas barks.

Thick-muscled men appear through the crowd, casting buckets over the side and then passing them in a line to douse the blaze.

"Oh, Percy. Oh, Percy." Sarah's voice trembles and her eyes dart everywhere, seeing nothing.

I grasp her cheeks, forcing her eyes to meet mine. They finally shift and hold.

"They aren't going to beat it; it is too far gone. We must get off the boat, Sarah."

Her empathetic eyes sweep through the elegant ladies. "Oh, Percy…"

I grab her elbow, forcing her along the tight

walkway running along the boat's sides. "Keep moving. They have lifeboats. There's no sense waiting; we will be last to board anyway. We are highly expendable."

She whimpers.

"It's alright my love. It's alright. Stay calm."

My eyes steal out across the moonlit water of the bay. Thank the heavens we are not too far from shore. The hair on my neck stands to attention. We are, however, in salt water. I am fully aware of the leviathans which glide unseen beneath the frothy waves. Especially on warm nights.

We leap onto the back deck where a few other less-importants gather, apparently of like-mind.

I bend down, sliding my hand under Sarah's skirt.

She slaps it away. "Percy, what *are* you doing?"

I shove them back under and my fingers continue on, searching for layers. I spin her round to unbutton her back, loosening the tight bodice which binds that beautiful chest. After a few moments struggle, I ease it off her.

"Jonesy!" Her face is all mortification. As are the few onlookers.

A few protests of, "Scandalous!" and "See here!"

I ignore them. My singular concern is to get her to shore alive.

"You will drown, my darling." I stare at her, letting my words sink in. "The clothes are much too heavy. Your strength shall give out halfway to shore."

Even in the dim light, I see the remaining color drain from her already-pale face.

"We are. We are swimming?" Her voice is incredulous.

She thrusts her head out to look at the lights of the shore, shining in the distance. She swallows, fanning her face.

"Yes, we must. And you must rid yourself of as much weight as possible."

Tears bead and flow down her cheeks in earnest, but she nods, lifting her arms to assist me. I helped her shimmy out of her layers till only her shift remains.

Scathing scowls change to terror as comprehension dawns on the onlookers faces. Soon the deck is littered with underclothes and waistcoats worth a fortnight's worth of wages.

We move to the railing. Screams erupt behind us like staccato bits of fear in the night. And the heat. I can feel the heat now.

Lifeboats splash to either side of the boat as Charleston's finest scurry over the side like common bilge-rats.

I pull Sarah back against my chest and whisper in her ear. "Miss Sarah Goodwin, will you be my wife?"

"What?" She whirls. Her eyes sparkle with astonishment "I. Well. Yes, yes of course I will."

Her warm arms wrap around my neck and soft lips press against mine. I squeeze her tightly for a single breath and push her back.

A few couples around us clap briefly and then cast off the side, splashing into the black water.

We clamber onto the rail, balancing on its edge. "Are you ready?"

Sarah gives a solemn nod.

"Together?"

We join hands, and leap—the shock of the cold

167

water seems to stop my heart. I sputter, feeling in
the water till I find her hand.

I sit on the dramatic four-poster bed, staring out
the window at the vast acres which comprise
Moreland. A flutter catches my eye and I quickly
stand. A curious netting is draped along the
bed's top and I reach up to slide it between my
fingertips.

"That's for the mosquitoes, Allegra."

I start, my heart hammering against my ribs like
galloping hooves. "You startled me, Lucy."

"Brighton says they're deadly. Carry all kinds of
pestilence. At night, be sure to pull them down
around your bed, for protection."

I swallow, staring up at them. So much I do not
know about these states. "Thank you."

"Come. I want to show you *everything!*"

"*Everything* is much for one day," I say, but
Lucy is dragging me behind her down the massive
staircase to the foyer.

She leads me to the porch where two large horses
wait at the bottom of the steps.

"We're going by horse?"

"Yes, silly goose. Couldn't rightly walk it. Not
in one day, anyway."

The large man holding the horse's bridle stares at
me. It's Toby.

He tips his hat. "Miss."

"Thank you."

Toby eyes Lucy with discerning eyes. "Miss

Lucy, take it easy on Miss Allegra. She may not be used to riding like you are."

"Oh, no. I love to ride—but thank you for the concern."

Toby tips his hat again and turns to walk toward the stables.

"Toby—"

"Yes, Miss?"

I nudge the horse up alongside him. "Might I be so bold to ask you something?"

He tilts his hat back to better see my face, his eyes wary. "Mam?"

"Did you not say Brighton doesn't believe in slavery? I'm. I'm a little confused. Are all those slaves I saw in the rice fields...paid workers?"

I see the light in his eyes lessen a fraction. "No, Miss. Brighton has his own, paid staff. Bought and freed from his father, by his own sweat."

"His father...doesn't believe in emancipation?"

His laugh is disturbing. Like a bow pulled at an errant angle across the strings.

"No. Brighton and his father...disagree on many things."

Lucy trots beside us. "Yes. Father threatened to cut Brighton off when he purchased his men's freedom. But Brighton didn't care. He left for six months and—"

"Miss Lucy. That information is a might personal. Perhaps he wouldn't want you—"

"Oh, no. Miss Allegra is his particular friend. He told me so himself."

One of Toby's eyebrows rise in question. "That so? Well, we still should let him share his own secrets, don't you think?'

169

Lucy's lower lip pouts but she shrugs. "If you say so."

Toby turns to go, speaking over his shoulder. "Best be back by dark Miss Allegra. Crocs, 'skitoes, and all sorts of badness lurk in them swamps."

"Thank you."

"Hurry Allegra! I'll race you." Lucy kicks her mare and bolts across the yard toward the thick live oaks.

I take a deep breath and follow—"Ha!"

Chapter Fourteen

The light is waning as Lucy leads me through thick clusters of Magnolia's lining the footpath. I shiver at their number, thinking of my recurrent dreams.

She's shown me the slave's cabins, the rice fields and a vast, stretching multitude of gardens and stables and truth be told...I am utterly lost.

Morelands is the largest estate I've ever seen in the colonies.

My horse halts of his own accord and I look up to see Lucy sitting rigidly atop her mare as she stares across a large pond.

My heart instantly beats faster and my chest burns. I bite my lip.

I'm quite sure my mother never saw this pond; at least it is not in her journal.

Spanish moss and Resurrection Fern snugly envelope the surrounding Magnolia's tree trunks like a lady's green gloves. My eyes steal to the heavens, sensing the impending storm. The air is dense, pregnant with moisture.

What remains of the sun cascades through the white blossoms, distorting and bending the light which bathes the ground in an off-putting color?

I stare and cock my head, taking in the hues. It's like walking through a dream.

"There's something...off about the light?"

Lucy turns to meet my gaze. "It's called the Violet Hour."

I must look confused because she clarifies. "The light is tinged purple. It's because of the Magnolia's. George called it, Magnolia Magic."

"George is your brother?"

She nods, but then her eyebrows pull together. "Bright has never told you about George?"

I think of the mention in her father's journal; "George's fits. I do this for him."

I shake my head. "No. When I met you and you spoke his name was the first I had ever heard of him."

"That is very very odd."

We are quiet for a few long moments as she stares across the pond.

Tears shine in her eyes, making them abnormally bright. "What is it, Lucy?"

"He comes sometimes, to the pond."

"Who comes?" I ask, my heart speeding up so fast the world tips a tiny bit. I think of the images, the smithy, my mother.

She swallows. "George. I miss him s-so much." Her lips tremble and she hides her face behind those delicate hands.

I ease the horse alongside her, so our legs touch.

I hesitate, not sure I want to hear the answer.

"What happened to George?" I gently prompt.

172

"Brighton says he's alive…just…somewhere *else.* I didn't believe him. I thought he was dead, like Momma. That Brighton was just trying to spare my heart. But then one night at dusk I came here, in the Violet Hour."

I must look confused because she clarifies. "It only happens twice a day; just before daybreak and twilight. When the night and the day pass by one another. And you need the Magnolias. Lots and lots of Magnolias to get the color."

A violent shiver rocks my body. My mind stutter-steps as I fight to find words.

"Brighton was gone, George was gone and Danvers *might as well* be gone, he never even looks at me. And…" Her breath catches as a sob chokes out. It's too sharp and deep for someone so very young. "George was like a child, but the most wonderful, mischievous child you could ever know. We did everything together. He. He…"

Her face buckles under the pain.

I understand and feel my own pain, hovering in my mind and my heart breaks open in my chest for her. Innocence never spared me pain.

Pain rains down on the worldly and innocent alike.

I grasp her hand in mine, and give it a little shake. "I lost my Momma, too. She was the only warmth in my house. In my life."

Lucy's eyes flick to mine and sharpen. She wipes the tears with the back of her and nods. "I've seen him…" she hesitates.

"I don't understand. *Where* is George?"

She points, *"There."*

"In the water?" I repeat.

The sour flood of dread fills my mouth. "I still don't understand, my dear."

Oh, but you do.

The burning on my chest becomes unbearable.

Thunder rumbles overhead as if The Almighty answers in her stead. A flash of blue lightning strikes, jumping through the trees, heading straight for us.

I grasp the reins and wheel the horse around, readying him to flee. "Lucy, come! We must go. This is not safe."

The searing on my chest is like a tiny bolt of lightning and I gasp, clutching at it.

It is *my pendant. My Magnolia pendant scorches as if it is on fire.*

I pull back on the reigns, fighting the horse's stutter-stepping, he trots forward—but Lucy is rooted. Shaking her head, staring at the approaching, sizzling bolts.

A blue flash. It strikes the Magnolia.

A blue flash. It strikes the shore.

"*Lu-cy!*" I urge the horse back alongside hers and yank the reins from her hand, hauling her mare around.

"No!" she screams, her tears streaming again. "I will miss him! I must see him!"

She slips from the saddle, flying in a whirlwind of white and lace toward the water.

"Oh my Providence."

I urge the horse to an instant gallop. Lucy's almost at the water. *If she falls in...and the bolt strikes...*

A blue flash. The lightning touches-down upon the pond.

The blue bolt connects, streaming on and on in a sparkling blue and white glittery current; like ground diamonds and sapphires have electrified into a malevolent star-dust.

Rippling waves of cornflower-blue resonate from the bolt's core, stretching in larger and larger circles—like a stone cast into a pond. They expand till one reaches the shore with a *thw-ack.*

A crush of pressure envelopes us, like an invisible bubble. The horses whinny in protest, ears lying flat, but stand utterly still. Mesmerized.

"Lucy." I dismount and gather her into my arms, unable to tear my eyes away. "Come away," I manage to whisper.

The stream of light ceases—its celestial candle gutted.

The pond ripples and I inhale sharply. Pictures shimmer on its surface.

"It's like God's Looking Glass," Lucy murmurs. "That's what *I* call it."

I gasp, hauling her backward, away from the water.

She pushes back, wrenching free of the cage of my arms. "*No.* Look there! Do you not see him, Allegra?"

A light sheen of sweat breaks on my brow and I squint. A young man appears on the surface, his hair the exact shade of Brighton's. I breathe deeply, trying not to swoon. He walks with an ungainly lope.

"*That* is George."

Lucy's face twitches with a contradiction of emotion. Tears stream to her chin but her lips curl into a tiny smile of utter joy.

She claps her hands then cups them around her mouth to bellow, "George! Oh Georgie, I miss you! Pleeeease come back!"

The figure makes no sign of hearing her plea. His slightly unfocused eyes stare at something behind him.

The now-purple light intensifies. I am wonderstruck. *Is this the secret in those books?* This is what Brighton seeks. I am certain of it.

His brother is lost. He's near mad to find him. He feels responsible somehow.

How does it open? Why does it open? Where *does it open?*

What sort of place exists, outside of our world? It looked not-quite our world, indeed like peering through the looking-glass. Our world in reverse. I squint, trying to make out George's surroundings. Flowers litter the field where he lopes.

The colors, the bulbs...are different, shades I've never seen before.

The light is fading. Someone unseen must call to George, because he turns, his eyebrows rising, limping toward a voice only he can hear.

"No. Please, don't go. Please, Georgie." Lucy crumples to the ground, crawling toward the electrified pond. I drop beside her, wrapping my arms around her torso, restraining her. Her fingers claw the wet dirt in her attempt to reach him.

"You can't go in there, Lucy."

She bats my arms, trying to wiggle free, her fingers outstretched—"I want to go with you. Please Georgie." Her chest heaves beneath my arms and her eyes are wild, as if she's talking to herself, not me. "It was always *he and I*. When

176

Poppa was mad-crazy, we would hide together in the oaks. Play together. I'd never-ever leave him. Let me go!"

I shake her shoulders and force her to meet my gaze. "*Lucy*. What would Brighton do without you? It would kill him to lose you, too."

I know these words to be true. So does Lucy, because she stops struggling, her body going limp as the hope drains away.

She stares, fixated, waiting until George's boot finally slides out of view and the ripples cease.

The pond is clear, and so is the air. No trace of the oppressive force remains.

Nightfall arrives in earnest; its inky black erasing all traces of the purple hue.

Toby's voice echoes in my head. *Alligators. Mosquitoes.*

"We must return to Morelands."

I drag her away from the water and ease Lucy back onto her horse and slap its hindquarters.

Lucy barrels ahead through the dark and if she weren't atop the white mare, clearly visible against the backdrop of the dark oaks, she would be lost. And so would I.

A loud snort issues to my right and I whirl in the saddle toward it.

A massive…bull-like beast with curlicue horns stares at me from behind a rickety wooden fence. Pawing the ground. It snorts as its nostrils flare, its eyes focusing on me.

Lucy pulls back on the reins and halts her horse, dead in place.

She's utterly still, but I see the terror and realization spread across her face. Her lips are moving frantically, but I can't hear her. She's too far off.

"Whoa." I try to halt my horse, but his ears lie flat on his head, sensing the danger.

The bull snorts in return, and *charges*.

Cra-aack. His large wooly forehead splinters the wooden fence like matchsticks as bits rain out, plastering my horse's chest.

"Protect me, Providence."

I whirl the horse about and kick his sides, digging my heels into his flesh.

The horse rears and the world upends. I swipe for the saddle-horn as the horse's front hooves leave the ground; it slips through my outstretched fingers and my bottom slides from the saddle to the horse's flanks.

I have just enough time to think, *I'm falling* before my breath whooshes out and pain jars my shoulder blades as my back strikes the dirt.

Black and white stars explode and pop like Brighton's fireworks in my vision.

"For mercy's sake, Lucy!"

Brighton.

I hear and feel hoof beats galloping to me and the insane charging-exotic-beast.

"*Roll*, Allegra!"

I shake my head in time to see hooves, backing toward my skull.

I roll and roll like my dress's caught fire.

More hoof beats, from the opposite direction.

"Toby, distract the water-buffalo. Lucy, go!"

Brighton's hands wrench me from the ground, into his arms and onto his saddle in what seems just a few blinks to my addled wits.

"Wrap your arms around me." I do my best, but my arms seem to have forgotten how to hold as he trots toward the main house. I allow my head to collapse against his back.

I struggle to remain awake, but vertigo spins the world like a Ferris wheel. The pace picks up and my stomach lurches with the motion.

"Allegra. Allegra," Brighton's voice soothes, thick with concern.

Despite my revolving mind, despite the bellowing beast, I am instantly awash in a warm, drenching relief. One repeating thought echoes through my head as we gallop.

Safe. I am ever safe with him.

Jonesy

"Must we return?" Sarah's hands fidget. We enter Charleston proper, its walls all but screaming of Yankee invasion.

The war is coming. People talk of nothing else. Those on the fence must choose their side, and make haste in getting there.

I slide closer to her on the carriage seat, so I may be heard over the rumble of the cobblestones. After swimming ashore, we managed to make it up the coast to a neighboring town, where we waited a few precious days. We visited a magistrate and became husband and wife. It was not what I would have wanted for her, but with Silas looming, I just could not return until Sarah shared my last name—so that I might have some legal recompense against him, should he try to harm her.

"Sarah—you understand what we discussed. War is unavoidable. We must leave Charleston. Return to my father in the North. But I cannot till I know Brighton and Allegra are safe. Can you? Say the word and I will force myself to leave."

Sarah's blue eyes fill as her face openly struggles with our dilemma. She blinks and a few stray tears fall. "No. I love Allegra like she is my sister." Her eyes are bright with terror. "Did you hear what he did to Mr. Peabody for botching the fireworks?"

The image of Silas's white cane, striking over and over invades my head.

A cold chill floods my veins and my eyes steal across the bay. "Yes. He disappeared. I expect he'll be washing up on shore any day now." As my one hand tightly grips the reigns, I take her hand with my free one, my eyes searching the bay. "I realize he's mad. We will remain one more week a fortnight at most—then depart and pray for the best. I hope the war can hold off that long."

We arrive at the dock and grasp hands tightly. I eye the isle warily. "We need to see if Brighton has returned to Fire Island."

CHAPTER FIFTEEN

Raised voices, filtering beneath the door, rouse me from sleep.

For a moment I am disoriented; the unfamiliar, ornate furniture immediately sends my heart fluttering like a bird against the cage of my ribs.

"I care *not* about succession. My sole care is to find my brother."

I sit up too quickly, which sends blinking stars of light dancing across my vision. I peer up at the gauzy-film of the canopy bed draperies, blinking and struggling…to remember what happened.

Is Papa on a tirade?

My skin crawls. For a moment I believe myself back home, in my opulent prison.

My fingers trail to the back of my head and I wince. *No, that isn't right.*

I stare stupidly at the mosquito netting. *Mosquito netting?*

This is not my childhood bed. My thoughts feel thick and weighted, like my mind has been dipped and coated in molasses. My thoughts drip in a maddeningly slow place to my lips and I grind my teeth against the slowly-forming-words.

Then sharp bark of Brighton's voice clears the fog away.

"Brighton," the voice next door rumbles, grim and low. "I have tolerated you doling out your inheritance to slaves, your refusal to run this plantation, and your fugue to join the circus."

"Amusement park."

Clear images form, sluicing through the thick treacle of my thoughts.

Brighton, the fireworks, my music. My memory rushes back in a litany of pictures. His lights and images, my sounds, married together in a perfect, mesmerizing display. Exploding in the night sky above Charleston's Fancy—a perfectly reflecting mirror-image in the bay below.

The hot surge of the Elementi through my extremities, healing my well-worn fingers.

The light and hope Brighton projects with every look. The feel and need in his kiss and his rough hands gliding across my skin.

"I love him."

It's the first time I've spoken the words, or even admitted it to myself.

"More than the sun and stars above."

I fell from the horse. The smell of the dirt and the wet thunk of my head against the ground returns to my consciousness—feeling as a memory inserted from another person's mind.

My newly-written symphony blares to life in my thoughts and I flinch in pain. The arguing voices are Brighton and his father.

Then something odd occurs.

A warm glow, like an ember, originates on my spine to crawl up my back, spreading across my shoulders, my neck, to envelope the goose's egg upon my skull. Like a gentle, invisible hand cradling the injury. I shiver as my mouth goes dry.

The throbbing dulls. My wits further clear. Fear surges through my veins. What have I done? What is this devilry I've ingested?

"Just bloody tell me how to titrate the mixture. I have tried for months. I know you open the passage without the poles. Have you no compassion, man? Care you not what happens to him? The boy is damaged but he is your *son!*" Brighton roars.

The warm, ethereal hand tightens. *The throb dampens to a small ache.*

"You foolish twit. George was the reason I began to experiment. To heal his afflictions. How was I to know it would become *so much more*? And to ignore such knowledge and opportunity is sheer lunacy, Brighton! The power. We will be *Gods.*"

The circular ache dissolves, its circumference getting smaller and smaller with every ragged breath.

And it is gone. The pain is completely gone. I rub it furiously, disbelieving.

The tingle at the base of my skull ebbs; its warming tendrils receding down my neck like an ivy-ungrowing, returning to seed. A seed in the center of my spine.

I am healed.

My mouth is dry as dust and I bolt to full-length mirror and lunge to snatch its silver-plated, hand-held companion from the dresser. I spin and hold it aloft, waving it to and fro in an attempt to glimpse the back of my head.

The voices behind the door drop suddenly and I strain to hear. I thrust the mirror back on the chest and pad to the door, inclining my ear against it.

"It is a cheat. *Enlightenment, true enlightenment,* and ascension to what follows, can only be obtained through the proper channels. Through purification of mind and spirit, and actions reflecting such. Over the course of a life well lived. And on a timetable not governed by the thoughts of imperfect man."

"*Bah.* I've labored my entire life and most often, do-gooders end up paupers or poets. I have provided this family with wealth beyond what I ever even imagined. And now I seek an even greater task…to give mankind an option."

Brighton's voice shakes, "That *option* is not yours to give. Nor was it your decision to inject George with the infusion. George was afflicted, but he was able to think. It should've been his decision."

The revelation moves up my chest to expand in my mouth, choking me.

George was simple. And his father injected him with *The Elementi*. From the sound of it a good deal of Elementi. If it had this effect on me…what would more do? What would happen?

I fight the swoon and slump into a chair beside the door, still listening intently.

"He is better off where he is. There is still much you do not understand, Brighton."

Crash! The pop and tinkle of glass shattering.

A small shard of crystal slides beneath my door,

skittering across the hardwood floor. It glitters in the morning sun, emitting tiny iridescent rainbows that remind me of the fireflies.

"Tell me, then. Leave George to me. *I* shall be the judge if he belongs where he is."

"Join me in succession, pledge your allegiance to Morelands. *Then* I shall tell you how to reach him. And stop freeing my ruddy slaves."

"Never," Brighton's voice shakes. "*People* are not possessions to be bought and sold at your whim. I will never join you. I will move North. Join the Union."

A dark chuckle raises the hair on my arms and I swallow.

Evil. His father is pure evil.

Brighton's warning echoes in my head: *He is a pitcher plant. Once trapped, there is no way out and he will devour you.*

My heart beats beneath the hand clutching my chest. We must away. Immediately.

"What about *her*?"

I step away from the door. My breath exhales sharply and I go rigid.

"Do. Not. Touch her."

A high-pitched keen of black laughter.

I scramble to my knees to peer though the keyhole.

Brighton's back quivers and his hands are balled in fists. His father is in a leisurely repose on a chaise, examining his fingernails. "She means much to you. I have sent out informants...to gather information. I wonder...if she has told you everything. About her past?"

"We are leaving."

"Take the powder again, Brighton. Perhaps then you shall see my point."

Brighton whirls, stalking toward my door. "You mean so I might join you in your madness? I was in error to take it even once."

"What about her. Have you given it to her?"

The tincture, dribbling through my lips. The swim in the salty pond. *The Elementi.* I have taken it too. *Bathed* in it.

What am I? Am I irrevocably altered?

I struggle and manage to upright myself but feel the press of the blackening swoon return. My feet shuffle backwards and catch on the rug and I manage a rough slump back into the chair—inhaling slowly, trying to keep at bay the darkness threatening my wits.

The door swings open and Brighton's hands are around my forearms. His voice drops to my ear.

"My dear. I realize you are in no condition to travel, but we are not safe here. We must depart."

He gathers me into his arms with such ease, as if I am a child, and whisks past his father toward the door.

As we pass, his father goads, "Miss Teagarden, is it? Good luck, Brighton. She is not as she seems. You know it as well as I."

Brighton slams the door with his foot so hard the plaster cracks, and hurries down the stairs toward the foyer without a glance.

Jonesy

"She must be found!" Silas grinds his teeth together and his eyes glow with a mad-sheen. Like an animal gone rabid.

"I *need* Brighton and Allegra to return. That blasted boat-travesty cost me a small fortune. If one of the gentry had perished that would've been the end of Charleston's Fancy. We would've folded. And you and your dear new Missus would be *sans* employment. Are you good for anything else, *Percival?*" His voice purrs like a taunting schoolboy. "Are those hands capable for more than pulling a bow across strings?"

My mind flashes to my past. Callouses riddling my palms, just like my fathers. Shovels, hammers and sweat; the sound of metal on metal. My father's promise my life would be different than his own of toil.

I suppress a bitter smile. *Silas always misjudges in his arrogance.*

"You instruct them to return—do not protest—you know their whereabouts. You tell them I shall send word to that very serious soldier that was skulking about not a fortnight ago. If I cannot have her...than no one shall."

I swallow and feel anger's heat flood my face. I bite back my words.

Money and power. *How will they fight against it?*

"Percival, you blooming idiot? Do you hear me?"

I nod. "Yes." I stand, heading toward his study door. "I shall make sure they know."

"And make it soon. I have orchestrated a grand ball planned to recoup the money lost from that fiery debacle. And I need their combined talent to awe the gentry and coax them from their coin."

Brighton tugs on the saddle-strap, checking its tension around the horse's middle. We will travel on horseback rather than carriage to enable us to avoid roads, if necessary.

"Brighton! Stop!"

Lucy bolts toward the stables, her dress whipping and flying behind her like the Confederate Flag overhead.

Brighton's face is unreadable, but his eyes are wide and indecisive.

Lucy skids to a halt, clutching his sleeve in desperation. "*Please*, you cannot leave me again. Don't leave me here, I'll go mad."

Tears well in my eyes and I press my lips together to keep silent.

"You are not my ward. If I take you, Father will press charges—anything to stop me."

Lucy's face screws up in horror. "No! You can't leave, you-can't-leave. Not again, Brighton." She sobs, her chest heaving.

My hand automatically covers my mouth to hide my trembling lips.

"I will run away. I will follow you." She whirls to me. "Allegra wants me, don't you Allegra."

I hold out my arms to her and she flies into them, gripping my waist tighter than my corset. I stroke the length of her glossy hair, and stare overtop her head at Brighton.

The pain breaks across his face. "Blast it all!"

He wrenches an axe from a nearby log and hurls it at a tree. It connects, imbedding in the bark with a woody *thwaack*. He stares at his boots, shaking his head, his face reflecting the indecision racing in his mind.

"I know. I know what you're missing about George," Lucy says, her voice partially obscured from pressing against my middle.

Brighton stalks over and drops to his knees before her. "What. What is it?"

"Aren't I as important as George? Do you love him better? Why won't you take meeee?" She wails.

"Oh, merciful father, Lucy." Brighton pulls her from my chest to his, cradling her. His face is raw with a heart-stopping mix of horror and pain. "Of course you are as important as he. It's *so dangerous*. Nowhere is safe now. At least here, if war erupts, you can hide—where I showed you, remember?"

Her blonde curls shake adamantly. "I can't stay here. No one loves me here, Bright. *Not like you*. Please."

Brighton's eyes meet mine, questioning.

My voice is hoarse. "I will protect her. The best that I am able."

Brighton's expression is black. "We shall remedy that as well. You will learn to shoot."

"Jones beat you to it, I'm afraid."

Brighton nods and then stares at Toby. "This will not end well. Send word if anything transpires when my father returns." And in an undertone adds, "To this time."

He follows Toby into the barn and I hold Lucy closer, willing my love for her through my tight embrace. "Shuush. All will be well, my darling."

The hitching of her chest and her small hiccups are her only reply. Her hands clutch the folds of my dress, as if in fear we shall change our minds.

Brighton leads two mares over and gently extracts Lucy from my arms, and he has hauled her atop the horse before I've managed to take two steps.

I slide my foot into the stirrup and swing onto the saddle, reeling with emotion.

Toby walks out of the barn and he and Brighton stare at one another, their arms bracing one another's shoulders.

My throat feels thick again. I've seen that look before. It's goodbye.

It was in my cousin's face before he left for war.

Why must life be so sad? So very difficult?

I grip the saddle horn so tightly my fingers tingle.

"Are you certain you can ride?" Brighton looks dubious. "Your head?"

I swallow and try to conceal the fear. "My head is...perfect."

Brighton swallows a grimace and nods, understanding my meaning.

Toby finishes securing the horse's halter and stares. "I don't know how much longer we can stay on at Morelands..."

Brighton nods. "I understand. Remember what we discussed."

"I am not taking that money."

"It's a *loan*. Just to get you and your family to safety. You take it, you stubborn ox. The papers I drafted will be respected by few. Keep to the swamp, travel at night. You have my contact in the North?"

Toby nods and swallows, tapping his temple. His great Adam's apple bobs.

Brighton extends his hand, and Toby grasps it tightly.

"My brother. I will find you through my solicitor as soon as I can. Godspeed to you."

"You bring Mr. George home and then high-tail it north. This." Toby's eyes flick away, over the fields. He nods to the flag above. "The days of this place are numbered. A blood-bath is comin. I feel it in my bones."

Brighton presses his lips together and nods. "Till we meet again. Go tonight."

Brighton turns to me. "Ready?"

I nod and Lucy and I follow him into the woods, in the direction of Charleston's Fancy.

CHAPTER SIXTEEN

It is near midnight as we arrive on the grounds. My cottage lies ahead, but curiously, no lights are on. Brighton quietly treads onto my porch and opens the door but no Sarah.

"Let us check Jones's cottage."

I smile as happiness and sadness mingle in a bittersweet taste in my mouth. I am thrilled if they have wed, and so very sad to have missed it. But in this life, this world, joy must be snatched and held tight when the chance arrives, as there is no telling how quickly it will end, and if or when it shall ever come again.

Lucy's eyes flit wildly about, trying to take in the still, quiet amusements as we pass enroute to Jonesy's cottage.

At last, we arrive and Brighton uses a singular knuckle to rap on the door.

Jones is there in a flash, his white smile lighting up the night.

"Brighton. Thank Providence." They embrace quickly. "Sarah is asleep inside."

Tears well and I wipe them, feeling foolish. "So you are wed. I am so very glad for you both."

Jonesy's returning smile removes years from his face. "Yes. She will be so relieved you've returned. But who is this?"

Brighton moves Lucy forward to stand before him. His large hands cup her shoulders, making her look even smaller, somehow. "This is my sister, Lucy. It is a very long story Jones—"

"It always is, Brighton."

They both chuckle quietly.

"It would be safer for her to stay here tonight. I do not wish for Silas to have yet another pawn in his game. I am sorry for the imposition—"

Jones extends a hand to her. "Do not be ridiculous. Sarah shall be thrilled. And I do miss my sisters." He takes Lucy's hand and leads her to the porch. He smiles gently at her, "I have three you know?"

"But my personal effects? They are still on the island?"

"I will take you there at first light, and leave you to collect them. In the evening we will move you here—for as long as need be," Jones replies.

Lucy smiles tentatively and nods.

"We will check on her tomorrow."

"Why aren't we going back to the isle?"

Lucy was now in the relatively safe possession of Jones, but Brighton was leading me away from the water, toward Charleston's Fancy.

193

We walk hand in hand down the thoroughfare. He turns to me; his mouth pulls up on one side, "Trust me. Do you trust me, Allegra?"

I hesitate. All my life I have truly only trusted women—my mother and Sarah. Never a man.

I stare at him; his deep blue eyes pull tight, waiting.

I nod and swallow. "Yes. I do."

His face breaks into a breath-halting smile. My ridiculous heart beats wildly in response.

"Good. I'm glad to hear that. Keep that in mind."

My eyes trail skyward. We have arrived at the balloon. He smiles even wider. "Up you go."

"W-what? I am…"

"Afraid of heights. I remember. Your face was alabaster at the top of the Shoot the Chute."

He works hand over hand, gripping the thick rope and with every tug the balloon gets leaves its heavenly perch, drawing closer and closer.

He steadies the basket and flicks open the door and I take deep, cleansing breaths, trying desperately not to swoon. "In you go, Milady."

My legs tremble so greatly I fear they will give way as I step up and into the basket.

Within seconds, he is beside me.

I feel the blood trickle from my face as the balloon rises quickly into the early morning sky. It is still dark, but will not be for long.

"Easy, my love."

His voice is thick and warm, and my mind is once again drawn to visions of us, intertwined. The best my imagination can conjure without any true experience.

He eases me down to sitting and slides beside

194

me, and we sit quietly for a few moments; the only sound in the sky the cry of the gulls as they escape off the bay.

"Allegra."

He gently grasps my chin to turn it to face him. A muscle twitches below his eye and his mouth is serious. His eyes steal back and forth across my face, as if memorizing every feature.

"I know not what the next days will bring. It is a dangerous time. I know not how I will fare. I know I have no right to ask. I am unable to provide you..." he stops, his voice shaking a little on the last word.

He wipes his hand with his mouth in a now familiar gesture of vexation.

I lean forward and press my lips to his to kiss away the concern.

They instantly part; his moan is deep and guttural as the fire explodes beneath his skin, incinerating my own. The heat on my chest and at the small of my back is a raging pyre as our elements sing to one another. Attract and draw us close.

I open my mouth and feel the velvet that is his tongue, lick my lips.

I wish to be his in every way. My mind screams at the impropriety but I boldly launch myself, just the same, to straddle his legs. His breath comes in ragged, hitching gasps.

His wide hands form around my waist and with a violent shudder he abruptly pulls back.

I feel my eyes widen and lean forward to find his lips again. I do not wish to stop. I never wish to stop.

195

"Allegra." He touches his fingers gently to my lips. "I. I love you. With all of my heart, soul and person. Though I do not deserve you. Nothing as good as you should ever have come within an arm's length of the likes of me. I wish to have you. Nay, I must have you. Please, put me out of this longing and misery and consent to be my wife."

Something sparkles in the rising sun, sending iridescent rainbows dancing across the brown of the basket—the colors remind me of a peacock's plume in the sun's rays.

My heart *swells*, so thick and full of joy, I fear I will swoon again. My throat is thick and tight with tears and I clear it. "I will." And then more boldly, "When?"

He slides the sparkling ring onto my finger and places his lips to it, trailing kisses from my ring finger to the back of my hand. He turns it palm up and kisses it again.

I feel his heartbeat escalate beneath my other hand, resting upon his chest. Brighton stops and fumbles with his waistcoat and I stare back, confused at the sudden shift of intimacy.

His fingers fumble in a pocket and extract a parchment. I cock my head in question.

"I. I saw a judge, and had papers of matrimony drawn up." His words spill out so fast then, I have to listen hard to discern them. "I was afraid something could happen at any minute—that we would never have the chance to wed. I know every girl dreams of a wedding, of white dresses and flowers and…and I imagine for you, it is all about the music…"

The confusion begins to clear and with it an all-consuming fire...of possibility. "You mean, all have I to do is sign it...and we are wed?"

Brighton's eyes widen and he swallows so hard I hear the click. "Yes."

I take the paper from his hand and see the pen in his waistcoat. I reach for it myself. My hand is shaking.

He notices and his voice is gruff, "I am sorry if I am too bold, too presumptive. To depart with you without arousing suspicion would be difficult if we were unwed. And I promise, when we have a different life—a beautiful party. With food and a gown and *you* may write the music and—"

I sign my name with a flourish and press my finger to his lips and his trail of promises dies to silence. The only sound between is our breathing.

We stare at one another. With awe. There are no restrictions.

His eyes rove over me with a new boldness, and I do not drop my own. I stare back and see the utter yearning reflected in his gaze.

He places both hand on my neck, and drags them slowly, to cover my collarbone and down to my dress.

He whispers, almost to himself, "You are so very beautiful."

His fingers stray to my buttons, and shake so badly he is unable to tend them.

He closes his eyes and his hands ball into fists. "Forgive me. I have never...wanted anything as badly as I want you. And now that the moment has arrived, I am *terrified* it will evaporate like so many other good things in my life."

I lean forward and place his hands on my face

and press my mouth against his to silence his worries.

After a few feverish, frustrating minutes, I am free of my corset and his fingers trail tenderly across my flesh and I relish the feel of the sunlight against my skin as it begins to stream into the basket.

I wish we could stay here, in this moment, and never leave. Suspend time indefinitely.

The next hour passes in a blur of tingling and tightening and the murmurs of my name and the feel of his hot breath.

His blue eyes steal to the sky. He kisses my neck tenderly and whispers, "Day is coming and our time is fading."

And then I hear it. The sound of boots crunching through the thoroughfare stones. My heart catapults, but from fear, not desire.

I gently shush Brighton and he stops still, listening.

I bend forward to peer through the tiny holes in the basket's bottom and see it. A white cane.

Silas stops, dead still, to cock his head…listening.

Brighton's fingertips sear hot streaks along my back, where he continues to touch me, despite Silas's presence. The desire all but screams. We are still as yet, uncoupled.

Please let him leave. Please let him leave.

I feel Brighton's hand slide up my legs and linger in tiny, excruciating circles, as my heartbeat threatens to ravage my chest. My legs tremble in a way that has nothing to do with fear.

Mercifully, a gull cries, breaking Silas's trance.

198

He shakes his head and ambles back toward the Guest House, walking as quickly as he can.

Brighton's body is immediately flush with mine. Our time is up.

Brighton voice is low in my ear, "I love you, Allegra. Always remember that."

With every motion of his careful hands, stars pop inside my head, reminding me of his seducing fireworks. How they called to me, even then…

And I exhale in exultation and with a shudder…as he makes me his wife.

The inner sanctum of Silas's rooms smells like a funeral parlor. The flowers are meant to soothe but are instead, cloying.

"Well, well, well. The Prodigal son and daughter return." Silas sidles up too close to my face, and I fight to stay still. Not to cower.

Brighton rushes forward, balling Silas's shirt in his hands to shove him backward. The buttons pop off at the force. "I will be having none of that. You have us over a barrel—but I won't be tolerating any more of your nonsense."

Silas raises a black eyebrow which seems attached—marionette-like, to his lips as one side elevates in a matching, lopsided smirk. "*Something* about you has changed." His eye rove openly across my breasts and I feel a hot flush creep the length of my neck to my face.

He tsk-tsk-tsk's his way back, swaggering toward me. "Miss Teagarden, have you relinquished your most precious commodity?" His eyes drop suggestively.

My face blazes, but I square my shoulders. If he dares to touch me again, *I* will strike him.

"Silas," Brighton steps forward, his entire body quaking. My heart hammers wildly—he will snap him in half.

"That, is not your concern," I retort, stepping backward, trying to put space between us, and to get Brighton away from him.

He doesn't need this devil's blood on his hands.

My flush deepens; so hot it's as if my face has been scalded.

"Oh, but Miss Teagarden." Silas begins to pace, smooth and silky like a predatory cat. "THAT is not your most precious commodity, is it?"

Fear tightens my throat like a slip-knot.

Brighton's eyes dart between us, confused.

"Miss Teagarden. I have had word from that particular soldier. Your name is not Teagarden. It is *Manners*. Katherine Manners, not only of minor nobility, but much, much more...a musical prodigy, who has toured all of The Continent, led and leashed by a proud, proud Papa." Silas smiles widely.

His eyes flick to Brighton and register his perplexed expression. *I should've told him everything, why did I not tell him everything last night?*

"As I suspected. Even you...you do not know her worth, do you?"

Brighton's gaze is wary and angry.

"Avoir l'orielle absolue."

"Allegra?" Brighton prompts.

"Perfect Pitch. You can play anything you've ever heard. You...are *Miss Mary Marvel*."

He knew I was a runaway, from a titled gentleman...but not that I was a minor celebrity. Making our situation infinitely more precarious.

I watch the recognition spread across Brighton's face, as he tries to work out the accusation. The posters littered Charleston—father's endless advertising campaign always preceded our arrival— like any great Carnival. And I was the freak, to be paraded across every continent, to replace all the coin my father frittered away with his bad investments and my brothers propensity for gambling.

I am the Golden Goose—only in my case, the Golden, freakish Songbird.

I press my lips tight to stop the tremble. "I have no idea what you're on about. You're mad."

But Brighton sees. He knows. But he recovers in a blink. "Stop detaining us, we apparently have a new symphony and show to create to relaunch your flaming boat of Hades, don't we?'

The amusement drains from Silas's face. "I shall *prove* you are Mary Marvel. And when I do, the two of you shall become permanent employees of Charleston's Fancy. Unless you'd rather me to send word to Lord Manners?"

Brighton stalks toward me, hauling me toward the door by the elbow. "You know where to find us. We shall be composing."

"And do not forget our sparkling accompaniments in the sky." His fingers twiddle like mock fire bursts around his head. "Be very careful with my investment, Brighton, she's merely on loan to you."

Brighton's hand shakes where it grasps my elbow, but he makes no reply.

He holds it with a mere two fingers but its force is like an iron caliper. He leads me, stomping through the halls, past the quizzical gaze of servants, his eyes ever forward.

"Brighton. Brighton, I. I wanted to tell you. You knew I had that ability, photographic memory for music—I told you—"

"But...Mary Marvel. Perfect pitch. *You* are the infamous Mary Marvel. How could you fail to tell me that? After last night..." A flicker of pain crosses his face, and is like a knife to my gut.

His expression hardens. "It's *astounding* you remained hidden. You've lost twenty pounds from the poster. And your idea for the masquerade...quite brilliant, really, to hide yourself." I hear the bitter tinge lining his words. "I cannot believe I did not recognize...did not conceive..."

"I'm sorry. I realize this puts you at a much greater risk. I should've told you. But you still haven't told me everything about George, even after last night. We're even. I heard you arguing with your father, and Lucy told me. I've changed since...the element. I can do even *more* than before. That night you found me in the tent...I can play every instrument. Every one with perfect pitch now."

"Be quiet, Allegra," he chastises, looking left and right for eavesdroppers.

I rip my elbow from his grasp and rub it to dull the ache. In his agitation, he has forgotten to curb his grip. It will no doubt bruise.

202

"Answer me, Brighton!"

"I am sorry Allegra. Katherine? Mary? Whatever I am to call you. Whoever you are. I detest deception."

"I am not moving till you explain," I huff and halt in place.

Several guests eye us curiously. He stalks back, grasping my arm again, too hard. I whimper.

His eyes dampen from fire to fear as he quickly releases my arm. "My strength is difficult to gauge, especially when I am...upset. This is neither the proper place nor time. Later, Allegra. *Please.*"

The placation in his tone punctures my anger and it whistles out, like a downed hot air balloon. "I am sorry too." I lean closer to him, feeling the waves of heat that radiate from his skin. "I am frightened," I whisper.

His eyebrows rise, but he offers no comfort. He says nothing.

Nothing on the ferry, nothing as we step onto the isle.

My stomach is churning with worry and doubt by the time we head into the ferns.

He starts down the path for the hot spring and retorts over his shoulder, "Please, do check on Lucy."

He whirls to head into the forest. I huff and stomp behind him, unwilling to be dismissed.

I am panting to keep up with his break-neck pace as he weaves through the Live Oaks, not looking back.

I stare up at the fading light. Lucy returned this morn to collect her effects and Jones will be here at any minute to take Lucy to the mainland.

Thunder rumbles and my breath quickens. It seems all the elements are in place as when I was with Lucy.

Will George appear?

The fireflies descend; swooping, floating sparkles of light against the inky black-backdrop of the tree canopy. I no longer fear them—I thrust out my arm and they descend, wrapping about my arm like a full-length, illuminated glove.

The back of my spine tingles and for a brief moment our heats combine to a pulsing, breathing being and I shiver.

They are blinking and speaking again. I don't have time to discern their message. I wave a flurry away from my ear and the horde takes flight from my arm as I approach Brighton.

Brighton stands, his back to me, facing the bubbling spring. His chest heaves—I cannot discern whether it be anger or sadness. My chest tightens to think of such a powerful man, crippled by this magnitude of pain.

I yank his arm, spinning him to face me. My eyes scan his face, trying to reach him again, to melt the hard mask dulling his eyes.

"*Tell me.* Tell me everything this time. You must. If we are to have any chance together—there can be no more secrets."

Brighton's eyes flick from the lightning to the rods to my face and back like a pendulum.

My mind registers the dot-dot-dashes and a word appears in my mind.

"Them," I prompt, pointing up to the lights. "They are saying, Stay. Stay." I bark a laugh. "That's amusing. They told me to go, before."

I startle as heat and fur assault my legs, a winding and purring whirlwind beneath my skirts.

Brighton's chest is heaving as his eyes jump across the water. The words pour out, rushed and fast. "Injured animals. I began with injured animals. Feeding them the element. They improved, miraculously. I was astounded; limbs regrew, old grew younger." His eyes tighten, "But it seemed, wrong."

I feel the burn of the element racing beneath my skin.

"It *altered* them. Increasing their intelligence far and away from any normal animal I had ever seen."

The cat's stalk the pool and meet my gaze. A decidedly shrewd expression on their furry faces. I could not place what was odd about them before.

I swallow. They *understand* our conversation.

Brighton walks the pool's circumference, shaking each rod, checking its stability, eyes never leaving the sky.

"It is not up to man to tamper with the hourglass of life." His voice sounds ancient.

I freeze as images flit across the pond, so quickly they could be mistaken as ripples.

Brighton begins to pace back and forth, like the cats.

"The fireflies?"

"More casualties to my madness. They merely landed on the pond's surface..."

I stare up as they perform a whizzing, sparking performance overheard; like tiny lighted acrobats contrasted against the black sky like an outdoor big top.

"After the animals off behavior, I had my

suspicions. Lodged in the center of my chest was a niggling doubt that refused to die. I found my father's journal. He had been feeding *large* amounts of the element to my brother. My brother who's wits had been addled since a childhood accident. He was like a child."

He stops. His shoulders slump and his face collapses as if the words have broken through the shell protecting his heart.

His eyes shine with wetness and he blinks furiously. "He was all that was good. Always happy, always giving. And. He…"

I walk quickly to him, whisking past the poles to wrap my arms about him, pressing my face to his back. I feel the rumble of his voice against my cheek.

"He…was better at first. Speaking and reasoning more normally, in a way we had not witnessed since childhood…but looking steadily less happy as his comprehension improved. Then, one night, he *disappeared*. Then my father began to disappear for long periods, with no explanation on his return."

I squeeze him tighter and feel his warm hand slide overtop my forearm.

Lightning strikes an arm length from my boot, hissing the ground; the fireflies alight and the cats bound for cover.

His chest catches and he issues a tiny groan. His words spill out, like a dam broken and rushing. "He refused to tell me what happened. So I left. George and Lucy were the only reason I ever stayed on at Morelands, to protect them. The Elementi doesn't just heal. If you ingest enough, you begin…*to become light.*"

206

I loosen my grasp to slip around to face him. "I don't understand."

His eyes are wide with wonder and fright. "Another plane. Another place. Many other places. It is not heaven, more of a sideways shift in time. Have you ever heard of a doppelganger?"

I shake my head. "No."

"Neither had I. It means, one *the same* as you. It is you. Only in another dimension."

My brain seems to squeeze, trying to fathom his words. "Another me? What is this..dimension?"

"My father mastered these...gateways. Some bodies of water are rife with the element—and are passages to future times, with more science. Father learned they propose that parallel places exist— alternate selves that may have chosen courses completely opposite to our own. An alternate reality of our choices. Or unforeseen occurrences."

My head rebelled against the idea. "This seems quite impossible."

Then a revelation hits so hard I almost double over.

"Brighton. My mother—the windows and doors. She *knew*. She somehow knew about them. She was trying to tell me, some were windows and others were doors...but to where? But the poles? I have seen the images without them?"

"Yes. It is all about the concentration of the element in the water. One needs the right concentration, the right current. If the pond has enough, no rods are needed. But for me, it happened during storms, the electricity in the air. I have managed to see the windows, but open no doors."

The lightning strikes again a breath from my

boot and the suffocating smell of weather and sparks and sea-salt permeates the pond.

"Allegra you must go. It is not safe. You now *attract* the lightning. It is drawn to the element within your skin."

"No not till you finish," but my legs begin to shake as the angry sky rumbles in warning once again.

"The element—my father believes it to be the one used by the Pharaohs in Egypt, before the knowledge was lost, or *removed* from them."

"That's what you meant by cheating."

He nods and swallows. "One cannot attain indefinite life, whether here or There—" his hand sweeps across the pond, "by this means. This knowledge was meant to be hidden."

"It still seems mad."

"Many realities are mad. The fact you can play anything you hear just once, even without the element. *That* is mad."

I nod and step closer. "It is."

He bows his head and his lips graze mine, softly at first. A desperate kiss, longing for hope. I inch backward and my heart falls to my stomach.

The world alters; shifts and drops. I whip my head in time to register my boot slide off the bank.

I plunge into the pond with a tremendous splash.

Brighton lunges forward, hauling me out the water as the first bolt collides with the rod. We stand, clutching one another, slowly backing away.

His eyes rove over me, searching for injuries as he gently wrings the water from my hair.

"The Element changes people. If one consumes *too* much, it drives you mad...like my father.

Perhaps a fail-safe, to stop mankind from using it."

The flickering in the pond continues, but the images are muddled, like a half-forgotten dream.

I hear Brighton murmuring in time with the flashes and growls of thunder. "One, two, three."

But the lights above are fading. The storm is moving away. The time between flash and rumble lengthening.

And then I see it. The pearly white of the oyster shell lying on the bank, an animal's supper, discarded.

Brighton follows my gaze, but even as his mouth pops open to protest, I stoop and boldly sweep it into my outstretched palm, holding my breath, awaiting the prickle and burn and tightening in my chest.

His eyes are wild and bright as he holds his breath.

But nothing. I give a tentative smile.

I exhale through my clenched teeth and manage, "You may pronounce me cured."

CHAPTER SEVENTEEN

"Lucy, please. Please be reasonable."

My sister sits at the scrubbed wood table, wringing her hands like a woman thrice her age. Her eyes are wide and frenzied, like an animal trapped.

"Don't you see, Bright? I cannot go back there. Please, *pleease*. Do not make me go back to him. There is nothing for me there. Just a bunch of ghosts rattling around that huge empty estate." She stands, pacing violently.

"War is coming. Allegra's father's soldiers inch closer every day. Silas is a madman and I am never here, ever on the search for George."

Her chest picks up the pace of her feet and then her voice catches. "When you *are* here, you see me. You look right into my eyes and ask how I am." She stands and walks around the room, dragging her hand past vials and pipettes as if they were the loveliest things in the world.

She paces faster and faster. "I shall go mad if you send me back. I will run away. Anywhere is better than Morelands. Your tiny cottage feels a palace to me, because there *is love* here."

I feel the prickle of rage spread from my neckline to my face.

How shall I ever protect her? What if I fail her, like I failed George?

Fear and pain are the true culprits; but my learned response is to channel any weakness into a *useful* emotion. So, anger it is.

I allow my head to drop into my hands and rub my temples. "Let me think, Lucy."

She dashes across the room and plops into the chair opposite me, leaning over the table to snatch my hand away from my head.

Our eyes meet and hold. "Please, my dear brother."

Reflected in them are a myriad of memories; a tiny Lucy, the highlight of my days after my mother passed on.

Her rolling playfully in the grass with George, like she was a boy.

Her picking wildflowers, presenting them to me, as a salve to my soul as miniature wars erupted between father and I.

She and George were my anchor to innocence.

A silent reminder of who I was before mother past, before my father went drunk with the Elementi's power.

I sigh. "At present, my only solution is to ask Jonesy and Sarah to take you when and if they depart Charleston. Till Allegra and I can...can give you a *safe* place to be."

She nods, but tears fill her eyes. "Without you. Without Georgie. I might as well be alone till I'm old and gray, because no-one, nowhere, will ever make me forget you."

I pull her onto my lap and wrap my arms about her, inhaling deeply the clean scent of her hair. As I have since she was old enough to toddle.

Bartholomew walks into the room, his gait growing stronger every day. My conscience prickles and I sigh. "Barty, I am off to the mainland. Please be sure Miss Lucy does not leave the premises, except in the company of Percival Jones."

He nods. "Yes, sir."

I startle awake to the sound of Sarah's gentle snoring from across the hall in the dark. She insisted I sleep here tonight-afraid I would disappear once again.

I have not told her about Brighton, something holds me back. And after the fight with him...I welcome the quiet space of our cottage, for what may be Sarah and mine's final night together.

I dreamt of puzzle pieces, filled with bits of lightning and fields where the downy flower heads were made of blinking fireflies. Magnolias, of course.

My mind refuses to let it go, even when asleep. The clues all fit together, somehow.

My chest burns and I scratch at it and frown.

The pendant is hot against my skin. Why? What makes it so?

Light flashes out the window and I hurry over to draw back the draperies and my breath catches.

The fireflies. They swarm about my porch, spiraling down the posts and along the railing like blinking decorative lights. They have *found* me. Dread fills my mouth. *They never depart the isle.*

I step outside and fight the vertigo that erupts from being in their ever-moving midst.

They *swarm* over me, clustering me from head to toe.

I remain very still, closing my eyelids as they congregate over every inch of my skin, stifling my whimper at the troubling, scratchy feel of their insect bodies. They are warm, but still too reminiscent of the whisper-walk of a million tiny spiders.

Without warning they depart, returning to their original position. The flashing strobe re-lights the porch.

I clutch my chest, catching my breath to stare at them.

A decided, *patterned,* repeated flashing. They are communicating once again.

Brighton said the element healed. And changed the intelligence of any being it touched. *What do they know, that I do not?*

I run inside, grasping my mother's journal and begin to scribble the pattern of dots and dashes as sweat forms on my nape and trickles down my spine.

The twinkling swarm takes flight and I rush to the railing, gripping it to stay upright. I *feel* their departure; as if when together, the element inside me, and inside them, meld to become one stronger field.

A thought chills my blood.

Am I drawn to anything...or anyone who houses the element?

Like human magnets?

The lights now bob and weave and flit down the thoroughfare, past the Guest house and out into the bay, heading back in a tumbling mass of sparkles toward the isle.

I flip open the Morse code book Jones procured for me and set to work. My eyes sting as the sweat pours from my brow and I dab it with my dress.

My fingers finish their decoding and I sit back, blinking, tilting my head in discernment.

I read it once again. To be certain.

"Come to me, Allegra. Mind the magnolias, child. They always keep secrets."

I drop the book as if slapped and shoot to stand, shaking all over. I clutch the porch rail and battle the swooning blackness.

Sarah appears at the doorway, her face the milky-white of fear. "What is it Allegra?"

"It's her. They brought a message from her. I must find her."

I stride into the bedroom with Sarah right behind me. "Please Allegra, what is going on? Speak to me?"

I whip open the armoire, my hand searching through the dresses till I feel the familiar fabric brush my fingertips. I haul the dress unceremoniously out and cast it across the bed.

"Fetch me your sewing kit, please?"

214

"Allegra—"

I grasp the Magnolia on my dress. The dress I wore the day I fled father. My only dress from home.

"I shall rip it if you do not make haste!"

Sarah bolts across the hallway to her room and returns with the kit, which she brandishes at my face. "Here. What is *happening?*"

I extract a tool and begin to pick at the stitches that surround the magnolia patch. I had to work diligently; my mother had been an excellent seamstress.

"Allegra, please!" Sarah's face in pinched in fear.

"You should fetch Mr. LeFroy. Tell him I need him."

Sarah huffs and stamps her foot. "I will not *budge* until you explain."

At her words the final stitch gives way. My breath catches.

Concealed behind the patch is a carefully folded piece of parchment. My mind races back to my mother scolding the ladies maid.

"Take care with Allegra's patches. Do not get them wet, the colors will run." Then after further consideration, "I shall wash them myself. Never you mind."

I smile and feel the sting of tears. "You clever little liar. Water would ruin the parchment."

"What are you on about? You are going daft." Sarah begins to pace, her dark red hair bobbing this way and that. "I always knew it would happen."

I extract the parchment and her eyes grow wide, resembling chocolate saucers.

My hands shake and my heart clenches, fearful I shall tear the paper.

I open the folds to reveal my mother's perfect script.

An overwhelming sense of joy engulfs my soul; like she is present, stroking my hair, murmuring her reassurances.

Indeed, like she whispers in my ear, from beyond her watery grave.

Tears spill over and I carefully place it on the bed and then wipe my eyes, fearful to smudge the ink.

"Is that? Is that from Lady Manners?" Sarah voice shakes.

I nod, unable to speak and lift it with the care I'd give a broken animal.

Allegra. I would never leave you without good-bye, my darling girl. So if you have found this, something has happened to me. My sketches. Visit the ones with the doors. Stay strong. I love you with every beat of my heart. I shall see you soon.

My chest heaves and a wail breaks my lips. It is like her hand is in mine, giving me the familiar, reassuring squeeze, our silent communication used so many times when under duress, the touch meant; *I love you. Stay the course.*

But what does that mean? That she shall see me when I expire?

I shiver.

I nod, tucking it away and turn to Sarah. "I do not understand what is happening. Much of what I've seen...I do not wish to endanger you any more than I already have, my friend."

216

Sarah's mouth works with unformed words, but her expression shifts. "Whatever you think be best. I trust you. We shall take Lucy when the time comes."

I hug her quickly and whisper, "Thank you. Please go find LeFroy."

I quickly scribble a poorly fashioned map, derived from my mother's sketchbook and thrust it into her hand. "And do give him this."

We hurry outside and in moments are breathing in the dense, night air.

Sarah squeezes my hand as we stepped from the cottage porch. "Allegra, please, please do be careful."

I look over my shoulder, already breaking into a run. "I will."

I tuck the sketchbook in my pack and bound for the pond.

One of the three ponds in Charleston, surrounded by Magnolias.

Chapter Eighteen

I run so fast my legs burn and protest at the pace, but I haul my skirts higher, bobbing and weaving through the tight forest path. The only sound of the early-morning air is my labored breathing.

The sun is coming up, breaking through the clouds; dim streaks of pink light break through the forest canopy.

A hot, tight breeze blows against my back. The sun will not last.

I worry my lip, searching my memory. My mother's tirade, the angriest I had ever seen her, when I had misplaced my earring.

"You must wear them *always,* do you understand me?"

She had shaken my shoulders until tears formed in my eyes. My mother was gentle as a doe; but that day, her fingernails dug like talons into my flesh.

I had found it of course. And lost one again on the day of my flight.

The burning in my chest becomes a hum.

I break through the clearing that gives way to the pond. My heart pounds in my ears.

I am struck with déjà vu. I recognize this body of water.

My mother had been here. Had seen it, had sketched it. We had been to Charleston two other occasions, while I toured. It must've been the first time she had captured the pond perfectly on parchment.

I flip open the sketchbook, rustling the pages till it appears.

A door is sketched at the bottom of the paper. And below it the words, *The Violet Hour*.

For a moment, the world shrinks to a pinprick and I stand still, sucking in the hot, dense air. Slowly the light expands, returning to my vision.

Lucy called it that as well. Had they met, somewhere, while we visited?

I search my memory, rifling through our trips. And a random thought presents itself. My mother, returning to my guest room, after wandering about, sketching. "I met the most delightful child and her nanny. She was by the water where I was sketching, and Allegra, you would so like her. She—"

And my father had walked in. She had not brought her up again, and truth be told I have never thought on it twice...till this very moment.

I flip furiously through the pages, searching, searching.

And. Very small, at the bottom of a separate page...is Lucy. A younger, tinier Lucy—but the resemblance could not be coincidence. She had met Lucy. Who had told her about the water? About the Violet Hour.

The sun blazes bright, streaming through the Magnolia trees.

The pond ripples as if shivering as the light gently touches the surface.

Sunbeams bath the blossoms and the clearing alters. A strange purple hue emits from the trees, through the bounty of Magnolias, casting itself upon the surface of the water.

The bubbling intensifies, and a low roaring sound, like an approaching cyclone, envelopes the clearing.

The scene with the Blacksmith reappears on the surface.

"With the Violet Hour, there is no need to for the lightning? The concentration of The Elementi is strong, here."

The searing on my chest becomes unbearable and my hands clasp the Magnolia pendant, ripping it off in my haste.

I toss it about in my palm. It burns. It is not my skin reacting.

The pendant is hot to the touch.

"I don't understand."

"What is going on?"

I jump at the sound of his voice. Brighton has arrived, his eyes adhered to the water's surface.

"Brighton, I believe it's a door." The revelation rings in my head like a bell. "A gateway, like your father said." Confusion twists my thoughts and I bite my lip. "My mother. She knew about them. She..met Lucy. It is why she drew a door beneath the water."

Images flit across the surface. A blacksmith,

striking and molding, shaping and melting. And I see it again.

"My mother's skirt." I thrust out my finger to point it out to Brighton. Brighton's eyebrows knit together. "But I do not understand. There is no lightning. I thought it only opened with the lightning, in ponds with large concentrations of the element? Causing a chemical and electrical fusion?"

Brighton's eyes flick back and forth across the surface and it see the familiar depth that appears when he is ciphering. "Give me the pendant."

I tip it into his hand and he holds it aloft. The sunlight bends; its beams seem to intensify and strengthen and separate, all converging to hit *the pendant*. His hand shakes as the rays grow hot, but he doesn't budge.

The violet color intensifies as the sunlight filters through the Magnolia blossoms.

"Your pendant. For the door to open. Don't you see?"

"No! What do you mean?"

The blacksmith has finished his task, and plucks a tiny something from a mold and places it in my mother's outstretched hand.

"Light has a frequency. Each color, its own distinct frequency. The color violet, a pond with enough concentration of the element will...also open the door."

"But George. I thought you worked with the electricity because—"

"The current does open the door. But only a certain voltage, a certain amount of The Elementi in the water. Lightning is drawn to the element, and

George…was so full of the Elementi…the lightning *followed him*."

"What?" My throat constricts.

My mother is handing the blacksmith a towering stack of coin, her palm closed around whatever he has placed there.

"Lightning struck him. And he disappeared while in the water." He nods toward the pond. "He traveled directly. There was nothing left of him."

"I was wrong. My way, we are dependent on so many factors out of our control. The weather, the correct pond. But your mother's way…my guess is the earrings have enough concentration of the element, to open any door."

His fingers closed around the pendant as the light streams from his fist, bouncing off the trees and onto the bubbling surface of the pond.

"But why does it not open now?"

"You have but one earring. You need the match."

The wind shifts and with it, the sun falters. It mars the image in the pond and I drop to my hands and knees peering into the water. "Momma. Momma how did you know? How did you figure it out?"

My mother's hand opens, and it the center, is my pair of earrings.

"She had them forged of The Elementi. To draw you to the doors. To draw you to her. She planned to leave all along."

My bottom lip trembles. "Merciful heaven."

Relief, like crystal-pure droplets of sanity, flow through my mind, washing away the ever-present melancholy of the past two years.

"She didn't drown," I sob. "She didn't take her own life."

Brighton's free hand drops to my shoulder and he squeezes it.

I whisper, "She didn't leave me."

"She must've planned on taking you with her. But the door must've opened, and she had to pass through."

My eyes lift to his palm. "She had them made in case I was left behind. Or if she died before she could take me—to show me the way. For the element to draw me. To escape father and my life of servitude."

My mind races back to the day of my flight. The unrelenting beck and call as we played all about Charleston. The urge to flee. It was all The Elementi. The ponds around Charleston, calling to the Pendant.

And my mother.

The pond rises up, an almighty wave, like an ocean swell rising then crashes so violently, we leap backward as water sloshes over the banks.

The light above flickers and fades; the color of violet giving way to the darkness of shade.

"The pendant is cooling," Brighton warns.

My mother's face appears in the pond, her eyes directly upon me. Her speechless lips mouths, "Find it, Allegra."

Brighton and I are both so lost in our own thoughts; we speak not a word as the boat skips back across the bay.

He lifts me out of the boat and into the shadows, letting his hand linger at my waist. I lifted my eyes to his and see the fire that was present that night I first played for him. I feel a different kind of fire burn and lick my lips uncomfortably.

He reluctantly releases me and tethers the boat to the dock but is quickly back at my side.

We join hands and start down the path toward the cottage.

Once under the cover of the trees, he halts. "Allegra."

His voice is gruff.

"Yes?"

His large hand cups my chin to tilt it upward and I feel my breath increase. His lips touch mine, gently at first, but then work feverishly, the need saturating every stroke of his tongue in my mouth.

He eases my body down to the hard ground and slides his atop mine. I feel every inch of his lithe frame and my breath is so fast I fear I will expire.

His lips find mine again and his hands wind in my hair. They move over mine with a heated fervor, a wanting, like I'd never, ever felt.

All fades to nothing. Nothing else matters.

Not lightning, not the orchestra, not even my music. All that remains is him.

"My darling," he whispers in my ear. "My fragile, perfect Allegra." And trailed his kisses down my neck to trace my collarbone. His fingers brush my across my pendant and I shiver, my skin tingling beneath every touch.

"You, your fragile heart. You give me courage."

He stops abruptly to stare, unsettling me.

"We…have *hope* now, you and I." His lips part,

224

placing mine in the space between. One of my legs steals up, naturally wrapping around his and he moans softly. My body merely reacts to his, and I follow its lead.

"I love you, Allegra. I am sorry. I was angry. I care not if you are the queen of England."

I smile under his kisses. My heart leaps and plummets and the sensation of flying fills me. Fills my heart to bursting.

"I love you too. I have for some time. But you already know that, don't you?"

"I believe from the first time you pummeled me with questions…"

His warm, large hands, slide up the length of my torso, burning their way across my stomach which contracts with his touch.

I shudder convulsively and push closer to him. He aches to begin our dance once again—but worry plagues my mind, and I push him back.

"Do you know what marrying me entails? My father is wealthy, cruel and bloodthirsty. He shall *never* stop looking for me. He will have you killed."

His eyes flick to the trees. "I do not fear him. He should fear me."

He lays his finger across my lips to quiet me. My heartbeat leaps and I struggle to continue my warnings. His presence dulls my fear.

He kisses me again, this one full of promises and devotion. Tears well in my eyes as the lump forms in my throat.

"We shall disappear."

I stare at him, my eyes ticking back and forth over his face, trying to discern his meaning.

"I mean to keep you. If that means I am no longer Brighton Moreland, then so be it. We shall become someone else."

His hand slips to my face, his thumb securely on my chin, caressing my jaw. His eyelids lower, covering half of his blue eyes. "Yes?"

The gathering tears spill over as I blink and nod, "Yes. Most definitely yes."

Suddenly, a caterwauling of cats that sent gooseflesh ripping across my chest.

He is instantly rigid, instantly hauling me to stand. "For every good word, what is it now?"

Rage replaces the tenderness on his face and his neck muscles strain as his head whips toward the cottage.

"Lucy," he whispers.

He bolts, grasping me by the hand, dodging low hanging branches and leaping logs without a backwards glance.

The cottage door is open, only half on its hinges. "Oh no. No. No. NO." Brighton lunges forward, ripping off the door in his haste to enter. It cartwheels into the trees, ripping a slice of bark from an ancient oak.

"Lucy!" Brighton roars, running into the sitting room. "Bartholomew?"

I hurry to her room, flinging open the door. Her clothes are missing; not a sign she has ever been here.

"Merciful father," Brighton's horrified voice echoes from the kitchen.

Oh please oh please not Lucy, please not Lucy.

I tear into the kitchen to behold Brighton, kneeling before...a still, supine figure upon the floor.

"Bartholomew. My friend." He reaches up gently to close the older man's lids.

"Who? What?"

Brighton stands, his chest heaving. His eyes *glow* with a silver madness, and I see the pale gleam of *The Elementi* shining through.

He strides across the room to the table which houses his vials and burners. He swipes up a vial and pops the top and tips it toward his lips.

I launch—into the air toward his outstretched hand. My boot swings up as I kick the vial from his fingers.

"Allegra!" he roars, wheeling on me.

The vial clatters, spilling into a potted plant. The green leaves shudder and elongate, growing, stretching for the cottage ceiling. Plump, round oranges sprout and grow from its now-large limbs.

"What are you doing?" I cry, my hands up, trying to calm him.

"I want to be able to rip his limbs off with my bare hands!"

Brighton's lips pull back from his teeth and he *snarls*.

My hands fly to cover my mouth and I back away, edging toward the door.

The madness.

Bright's face falters as he registers my fear. His shoulders slump but his hands remain in tight fists.

"My darling. I am so very sorry." His chest heaves and the words stutter out.

He opens his arms to me and I rush forward without hesitation.

He is trembling all over. Or is it I?

"Who took her?" I mumble into his chest.

227

His hands stroke my hair, a motion that seem to calm him as much as it does me. "It was either Silas or my father. Which is like choosing between demons."

I pull back.

His eyebrows knit in a dark line. "We need to go. We will go to Charleston's Fancy first."

CHAPTER NINETEEN

Allegra's eyes are wide with fear, but her shoulders set with determination. My love and pride for her swells, and a deep gratitude, that someone so deeply good, could love the likes of me.

I stride down the thoroughfare with all the self-control I can muster.

Heat radiates from my spine; billowing out to my arms and legs in a never-ending pulsation. The abnormal strength is difficult to tether. I oft find my fists flexing of their own accord. As if my appendages were mere marionettes to The Elementi.

I grind my teeth at the need to destroy something, *anything*.

The cool touch of Allegra's hand on my arm slows my pounding heart and lessens my lock-jaw by a fraction.

"Easy, my love. Many are watching." Her voice, like her music, is warm and smooth as honey.

She struggles to keep pace with my strides. She is right, workers eye us as we pass-dropping their stares when I glare back headlong.

I stride into the Guest House, past Silas's security.

"Mr. LeFroy? Mr. LeFroy, do you have an appointment?" the guard prompts, hurrying out from behind the counter.

I whirl on the stairs and he halts, taking a step back as he stares at my eyes. Which I know, glow with The Elementi.

"I. Am going to see Silas. I do not recommend you interfere, Charlie."

Discretely, Allegra moves past me on the stairwell, out of his reach. She now hurries up the stairs and down the hallway without waiting.

I catch up and pass her to throw open Silas's study door.

A woman screams and bolts into a neighboring bedroom.

Silas stands, a wicked smile twisting his lips as he rearranges his disheveled clothes.

His voice is tauntingly serene, "Mr. LeFroy. Miss Teagarden. Welcome home!" He spread his arms wide.

Allegra shivers beside me and I fight the urge to wrap my arms about her.

I will myself in place, trying to halt the disturbing images invading my brain.

I am very, very close to ripping Silas limb-from-limb.

The problem with this frequently over-used phrase is with The Elementi, this is an all-too possible reality.

"Silas. Where is Lucy?" My teeth chatter with the fettered rage.

His sickly smile widens. "My, she is a precious

peach." Lust colors his lips as he gives them a quick lick. "Just ready to be *plucked*," His lips popping on the p sound.

I launch at him.

Allegra pelts her tiny body between us, her hand pressing against my straining chest like a butterfly's wing. "That is what he wishes, Brighton. Do not give him a reason to hurt her."

Silas's eyebrows rise. "Perceptive, Miss Teagarden. Now shall we talk contracts?"

Silas hauls open a desk drawer to brandish a parchment, which he thrusts into my hand. "This document binds you and Miss Teagarden to Charleston's Fancy for as long as I am inclined to have you in my employ."

Silas places the pen into my hand and a squall erupts in my soul.

My digits twitch, and the pen shatters into a myriad of fragments, skidding across his hardwood floor.

His eyes tighten; not with fear, but with discernment.

Allegra steps forward, distracting him.

"Silas, be reasonable. Even if you have Lucy, which we have no evidence that you do, we could not possibly bind ourselves to you indefinitely."

"Oh, my beautiful dear," he tenderly croons, reaching up to stroke her cheek with the back of his hand. "I *do* have proof."

Silas stalks back to the desk and opens the drawer once again. He thrusts his hand inside and for a moment I am perplexed...I tilt my head.

Gripped in his dark palm are two long, ebony braids. Lucy's braids.

I see nothing. I see everything. My vision swims with the color of blood.

I register crashing and screaming and a detached, moaning pain. Madness has arrived and eaten my reason and soul.

"Bright. Bright, stop!" Somewhere Allegra is shrieking. "We will never find her! Stop!"

Allegra's sobbing pulls me slowly back, back, back into my body.

Back into my right mind.

Shattered vases and crushed glass are spread everywhere, as if the hardwood floor has given way to a glittering ice rink.

Silas's skull is in a headlock. *In my arms.* My teeth rattle with a violent shudder.

I have no memory of how I've managed to subdue him.

I release the cad, and shove him away from me—he sprawls on his expensive carpet, now crimson with his own blood.

Allegra is instantly pressed against my side and I lift my arm to embrace her, welcoming the calming coolness of her body.

Silas looks up, murderous. He rises, wipes the blood from his mouth with the back of his hand, never dropping his gaze. "If you ever touch me again, *she* is dead."

He walks slowly back and forth, evaluating us. I'd seen him examine horseflesh in much the same fashion. And that is what we were to him; *possessions.*

"I don't know how you've come to have the strength of ten men...but I shall find out. I assure you."

I grasp Allegra's hand and head for the doorway. "We will not sign. If you kill Lucy, you have nothing to hold us here. We shall return tomorrow, with something written. On the night of the performance, we deliver the arrangement, and you deliver my sister. Otherwise, your skull crushes as easily as that vase."

I kick a shard and it sails across the room to land at his boot.

Brighton stares out my cottage window at the frenzied comings and goings of Charleston's Fancy. We have vowed not to move, till the new orchestral arrangement is complete.

His blue eyes pin me to the chair. "You need to compose. We need the music as barter for Lucy."

I nod and swallow, thinking of our first day alone. Of the inspiration his fireworks held for me, when first I saw them against the night sky.

"Draw for me." He continues to stare out the window, statue-still, so I add, "Draw what you're thinking. Make it into fire."

His eyes whip to me and I hastily add, "What choice have you?"

His jaw tightens. "None."

Brighton sits at the desk and sets to work, his hands sketching and angling and twisting so furiously, I expect the parchment to tear.

Anger. My music must match his anger. I bristle. I avoid anger whenever possible. I do something unthinkable. I open the memory gates which house my father. He stalks through them, through the mists of my mind; his black hat and great coat damp with English rain.

My fingers touch the cello's neck and the dance begins.

My fingers gyrate and *hold* on the strings, my other arm sawing, sawing against the cello's heart.

My father's hand, striking my face. At two, at ten, and the final time—when I fled.

The pull and burn of *The Elementi* against my chest.

My nostrils flare and the sounds in my heightened hearing echo; magnifying, bouncing off every nook and cranny like a grand hall's acoustics.

The wet blast of my father's drink in my face, streaking down my cheeks, down into my décolletage and the laughter of his bawdy, drunken earls.

"Why, my dear, can you play so beautifully, but are so bloody dense?"

The rough tap of his finger at my temple. My inability to respond.

The whole-body shaking begins—fury, helplessness, desperation and futility funneled into the quivering of every muscle.

All fades to black.

My space and time and reason is the vibrating conduit between my legs; as if the instrument burrows an avenue to my soul, spilling every vile memory where it is reborn as notes and tones and dissonance.

Staccato beats of strings. The sounds. So many sounds. Since The Elementi entered my body, my hearing is tenfold.

Amidst my music, I discern birdsong, the ebb and flow of the tide, hushed whispers down the hall...and...I cock my head.

The piece reaches the crescendo...I blink repeatedly. It's as if my father's drink has time-traveled, materialized on my face, somehow?

Strong, rough fingers stroke my cheeks. My eyes flick to his, but the music has captured me, and I must finish in my spellbound state. It will not release me till the final note is played.

Brighton grasps me under my chin, whispering, and "My darling. You are safe. You are here with me."

His thick finger strokes my eyebrow, tracing one to the other, sliding across my temples to trace behind my ear, down to my collarbone. His touch is firm, but controlled. I know it to be difficult for him to manage.

Father's voice again. The hot strike and sear of a conductor's stick against my back.

"Expressivo!"

Play expressively. He means play expressively.

I am the family's everything: our past, our future. Our coin, our livelihood, all riding on the back of a tiny seven-year-old and the notes she squeezes from her tortured mind.

A choked sob and a fresh reprise of tears, each drop an encore of pain and memory.

"Shh. Shh." Brighton kneels before me, his hands about the cello's neck, trying to extricate it from my frenzied fingers. "Shh. Allegra, come back to me. Leave that black place in your mind."

He tugs roughly; I release the cello and the music ceases with a jangled halting of strings. The silence in the room is deafening.

He eases himself into the cello's place between my legs and gently kisses my cheeks. Soothing murmurs escape his lips, each word bathing and tending my wounds. "Never go there again. Please."

I sob and nod and allow myself to be folded into his warm embrace. His hand slides up to cup the back of my neck. After a long moment, he eases me back out of his arms to stare into my eyes. I whisper, "The Elementi heals physical pain...but not the soul."

Brighton's voice is gruff, but determined. "The piece is...breathtaking. And heartbreaking. Are you able to remember it?"

I roll my eyes and he laughs loudly. The first laugh I have seen in weeks.

He grasps my hand and leads me to the writing desk. "Transcribe it for the rest of us. But please...do so without bringing back the source of inspiration."

I begin the blackening of notes between the lines and grind my teeth.

I whisper, "This is the last bit of my soul that beast shall get from me. For Lucy."

Brighton nods grimly. "For Lucy."

CHAPTER TWENTY

"Do you hear that?"

Brighton eyebrows pull together in vexation at my question.

"Of course you don't." I cock my head and stride to the window, inclining my ear.

A trickle of sound, playing and calling through the wind.

My newly-forged ears discern discrete tones; individual voices recur, bouncing through my mind like a musical refrain.

I whirl to stare at him, my breath matching my beating heart. "Lucy. I can *hear* her."

Brighton's face drains of blood and he reaches for the wingback to steady himself. "You *hear* her? What is she doing? Where is she? We must go to her."

His grip tightens, pushing down on the chair and I hear a *snaap*.

"Brighton. Your hands."

He stares at his hands as if they belong to another—but quickly shakes his head and releases it. His eyes remain unfocused so I continue.

"It isn't like that. I cannot discern words. Just the...tone of her voice. It's the timbre." I bite my lip, fearing another tirade. "I believe she was...crying."

Brighton shakes his head angrily; I watch, enthralled as the hopeful openness of his expression hardens into his usual mask.

His hands firmly grip my shoulders, and he steers me back toward the open window.

His deep voice is at my ear, "Listen, my darling. Find her."

I close my eyes, trying to keep the cacophony of sound at bay.

Intonations abound. *Birdsong*—variant and vibrant, hundreds of unique songs issued from individually-formed beaks. I push them aside.

The sea. The roar and whisper of the tides. I submerge them.

Insects—the buzz of bees about the white garlands surrounding the guest house. Smothered.

If I allow the din of sound free reign, I will most assuredly go mad. *My heartbeats wildly.* Each and every breath, sigh and laugh would become a continuous pressing drone, paralyzing me.

My world is now an auditory fabric, each individual a weave in the constantly undulating tumult of sound.

Brighton senses my hesitation. "All is well. You are well. *You* master *it.* Find her, Allegra."

I shake my head and plant a picture of Lucy firmly in my thoughts. Her ebony curls and long dark lashes, hiding those round chocolate eyes. Her throaty laugh.

I swallow and press down the cacophony till it is a low roar.

Her voice arrives, arising and undulating as a silver sparkling thread, standing out and shining above the drone below.

I bear down and I feel the vibration of the silver thread, weaving through the air—an auditory trail of breadcrumbs. I smile and feel Brighton's grip tighten.

"Ouch."

"I am sorry." He releases my shoulders.

"I can find her. I...have a trail."

His mouth turns up in awe and relief colors his features. "Show me."

"This night, all needs to be perfect. Do you understand me, Mr. Jones?"

Silas stalks before us and Sarah quivers beside me.

"I wish to see Allegra. I refuse to help you anymore until you take us to them. How do we know they are even here? Or alive?" Sarah's bottom lip quivers.

We have not seen Allegra nor Brighton since they disappeared the other night.

"Mrs. Jones. I assure you, your friend is quite safe and quite well." Silas walks back and forth in our bungalow, swinging that blasted white cane. I imagine pinning him to the ground, pressing it against his windpipe.

"After all, one day, I intend Miss Teagarden to be my own. Why in the world would I harm her?"

"She will never submit to that. Give herself to

you," Sarah spits, then quickly covers her mouth.

Silas's eyebrows rise and eye me menacingly. "You would be surprised what one would do...or sacrifice, on behalf of one's friends. Or lovers."

The hairs on my arm rise. *Devil.*

A protective surge rises in my chest—like that of a brother for a sister.

You shall not lay one filthy finger upon Allegra. I vow it.

He continues staring at Sarah till she squirms in place, "I need not her love. I merely wish to possess her. Love is for the weak-minded. But I would not expect either of you to understand that."

He lunges like a cat, yanking Sarah into a stronghold. A silver knife glints, pointed at her shapely throat. I freeze.

"You see, Jones? Your love for her makes you vulnerable. Makes you weak." He releases her, shoving her roughly so she stumbles and I catch her in my arms.

Seething, violent hatred pulses through my veins and I vault at him.

"No. No. That is what he wants, Percival." Sarah clings to my arm and I halt, chest still panting as I attempt to control the blinding rage. Her fingernails dig into my forearm.

"Continue with the masquerade preparations. The gowns, the food, all must be perfect. The Governor is set to attend. And I suspect some other royal guests."

Plimpton had mysteriously arrived yesterday with an arrangement whose style could only be from Allegra. No Allegra. No Brighton.

"We've only had the new symphony a day. You

are mad to play it so soon. Many of those musicians are new to Charleston's Fancy, "I protest.

He twirls the end of his moustache. "I am quite confident between yourself, blustering Plimpton and Miss Teagarden, you will carry the show."

Sarah sighs in relief at her name. That we shall soon see her.

The whinny and clip-clop of arriving horses on the cobblestones bade us all stare out the window. A large party has arrived on horseback.

I squint, trying to make out the newcomers, but Silas steps in front of me, blocking my view.

He backs out the door, wisely not taking his gaze from mine. After the door is shut, Sarah bursts into tears. I pat her, but stare through the drapes, to see if I recognize the party, but they have all swiftly moved out of sight.

"I have had a letter from Brighton."

"What? How?"

"The little boy. The one Allegra gave lessons to?"

"Yes?"

"He brought it round not an hour ago. He wishes us to take and hide his sister."

Sarah's lips pursed. "I do not understand. We saw her early this morn?"

I place both hands at her elbows. "Silas has abducted Lucy, and they have discovered her location. And...they wish us to keep her with us, till they find safety. To keep her from harm. If they deviate from Silas's directions, it will reveal their plans. But...he isn't watching us so closely."

"Where are they going?" she whimpers. Sarah's eyes fill and spill over as she blinks.

"He didn't say. They may not know."
"Do you really think they are safe?"
"No one is safe while that man walks the earth."

Next eve

I sit in my orchestra chair upon the riverboat deck with Déjà vu strong and cloying in the hot air. The new boat cost a small fortune, one Silas was no-doubt, anxious to recoup.

I run my fingers through the curls in my hair. Brighton assisted me in dying it black to further my disguise—we look more like brother and sister than husband and wife.

My scalp tingles remembering the feel of his strong hands in my hair as he massaged in the color. We sat in the warm bath, my back draped against his chest. I flush despite the fact we wore our small clothing.

The ways of husband and wife were not wholly unknown to me. My mother was sure to explain it to me before she disappeared. Though some of the dance remained mysterious. I find myself pondering it despite the danger.

My face blushes hot beneath the masquerade mask. Brighton's touch makes my normally shy disposition evaporate. I picture my body as a flower, opening and blooming only for him.

I stare down in contempt at the dress Silas insisted I wear. It is magnificent, no doubt, but wholly at odds with who I am.

My black-gloved hands smooth the dress of black and white brocade with patterned ivy, twirling across my breasts. Blood-red roses appear here and there through the swirls, to match the red silk center of the gown.

I shiver. They remind me of drops of blood.

A jewel-encrusted mask with long black feathers fanned about my face, matching the black of my hair.

"To better hide you, my dear," Silas had taunted.

I thought it was more likely to wield his power, to dress me like a doll that he soon wished to possess.

I shiver as my eyes scan the hillside. He will kill, at least *try* to kill Brighton at the drop of his top hat; I know that for a certainty.

I will not, cannot, allow that. I will die before I permit that.

To give my life in exchange for love…a love that fills my soul to bursting, makes me believe in myself as I never thought possible and has turned my inner despairs to hope.

To die for that kind of love…would be right.

"Above all things, we must have hope," I whisper.

The chair beside me scrapes the wooden deck and I gasp and summon every bit of self-restraint not to throw my arms about his neck. Jonesy.

He sits quickly, his black eyes narrowing and roving over me as if checking for injury. "My dearest peach." He sits and squeezes my hand tight leaning in to be heard, "Words do not express how relieved I am to find you here."

"Jonesy, "I breathe. "Sarah, is she well?"

Jones's eyebrows rise playfully. "I should not

tell you this, but I know you may away at any time. She is…" his eyes drop to my belly.

My heartbeat leaps to triple-time with elation and a twinge of jealousy. "She is *pregnant*. On my word, how wonderful…"

"And terrible. We, too, must escape Charleston's Fancy."

"And Lucy?"

"We have her, safely hidden, ready to depart."

Droves of costumed patrons spill onto the deck. This masquerade seems decidedly more macabre than the last. A man, his mask a long, sinister, sequined beak swishes past us, followed by a woman seemingly made of gold.

Her mask-top elongates into a many-branched, pointy money-tree, which towers over her head like threatening horns.

I shiver. And feel it. The heat on my chest.

The Elementi's draw.

Dread thumps through my chest, like an overture to impending pain.

Where is it? The water? What is drawing the element?

The bay has never drawn the element before. If it contained the element, surely so large a body of water would be unable to form a high enough concentration to produce a portal?

"Where is Brighton?" Jonesy prompts.

I nod to the hillside. "Back at the pyrotechnics."

"What is your plan?" Jonesy requests, removing his violin from its case. Maestro Plimpton has boarded the boat, looking like a rotund water buffalo rather than his intended costume of a Viking.

"For now, to survive this performance. We are still planning. Nothing is decided."

He nods, indicating the deck. My heart sinks. Sarah, standing tall and beautiful on the deck. Even at this distance, I can see the tears on her cheeks.

She lifts her long-fingered hand in farewell.

I wish to blow her a kiss, but fear others will notice.

"Oh, my dear girl. Please, tell her I love her."

Jonesy clears his throat. "You tell her yourself. The cruise is but an hour."

The final patron boards, the deck so crowded I'm worried the mighty boat shall capsize.

Silas climbs to a newly erected stand and raises his hands for silence. The excited voices drop to whispers.

"Welcome to Charleston's Fancy. While the country bickers over succession, slavery and sin, I give you this one night, a respite from all your worries. I implore you to lose yourself in the *dream* that is our establishment."

Thunderous applause erupts.

"Here, here!" yells a man nearby, holding up his drink in ascension.

"Without further ado. Please direct your eyes to our amusement park. Our Shoot-the-Chute will be open to the public tomorrow, so I recommend you stay at our very own guest house, to get an early start to assure your seat. And afterward, a ball, to begin at the stroke of midnight."

A hundred sets of masked eyes stare across the bay. I swallow.

Something, something is afoot. I cock my head to listen.

A whining hum, like I've never heard before, is an undercurrent of sound.

"How better to dance your troubles away than…with light!"

He flips his hand, and like magic, the whole of the shore alights. Dotted bits of light shine across Charleston's Fancy as if he has stolen the stars from the night sky. Stronger than lantern light.

Jonesy leans over once again. "I have never seen so much light at one time. I worry it is not safe."

My mind wanders a few months back, which seems like a lifetime, to Silas and Brighton arguing on the thoroughfare. A flash of Brighton's words, *'My father traveled to other times, with more science. Our time is not ready for what lies ahead.'*

Jonesy's eyes tighten as he stares at the shore. "It will never work."

Snippets of their argument return to me, now making sense.

'I have seen you do it. Seen you use such devices. I want them here. If no one else in all the world has them, we will become a worldly spectacle.'

Brighton had confessed his father, who used the portals without consideration of consequence, had stolen the idea from a man named Tesla.

He intended on introducing the light earlier, to further imbue Morelands with coin. Consequences to space and time be deuced.

I press my lips together, praying the world around us shall not fold from some untold time paradox.

Plimpton raises his baton and taps it for attention.

The crowd hushes. My chest sears and I whimper, but quietly.

Only Jonesy's eyes flick to mine. Sarah is gone. Tonight, Silas will keep the boat docked, to allow the curious to come and go between the performance and the magical lighting of the Guest House.

I raise my eyes to the sky and wait. A very long moment drags on.

Just as I hear the intake of the crowd's breaths about to murmur as to the delay, the first white jet shoots across the blackened night sky.

I pull my bow across the strings and the dance begins. My eyes never leave the sky, not needing my sheet music, only needing the synchronicity of Brighton's beautiful showers of light which ride on the wings of my notes.

The rest of the orchestra hums to life and I hear and feel violin, and horn and shudder with ecstasy. The Elementi's enhancements; the experience of sound is now sheer jubilation.

Blasts of cornflower blue and deepest purple pop and fan as celestial flowers in bloom above us.

Our music matches; every burst of light a staccato blast of sound, every showering light-rain, a smooth, slow adagio.

It is like the perfectly timed rhythm between man and woman. One who reads your soul as well as your body.

My mind tries to stray.

"Katherine?"

That voice?

No, it cannot be. A shudder of revulsion alerts every inch of my body to terrored attention.

I shake my head, ignoring the wildfire of gooseflesh erupting on my bow arm. *It cannot not be.* The burning in my chest is a hot coal of pain and I wrench it out to rest upon fabric instead of skin.

"It is *she*. Katherine!"

I keep playing but whisper frantically. "Jonesy. Oh merciful heaven Jones, he is come. My father is come. Save me."

Jonesy halts, taking the violin from beneath his chin, his eyes wide with fear.

Silas notices. His eyes have never left my face since the song's beginning.

His mouth twists in fury and he hops from the platform, snaking his way through the crowd toward us. The orchestra and music plow forward without me.

The floodgates of dread break. Hands grip above both my elbows, hard enough to bruise as I am hauled away from Jones, who is swinging, brawling like a wildcat.

Plimpton notices but conveys the rest should keep playing.

My eyes lift slowly to behold my father's maniacal, dead gaze.

He grasps my one arm, my brother the other, as they drag me toward the back of the boat.

The soldiers brawling with Jones leave him as my father walks away. Following loyally in his wake.

Jonesy hesitates, the indecision reflected in his eyes which flick between me and the hillside. He sprints in the direction of the fireworks, no doubt to summon Brighton. He will not make it in time. I shall be gone or dead.

We are alone on the back deck, the other patron's enthralled with the show and the magical lighting of the house.

Father shakes me, hard enough to rattle my teeth. His eyes ticking to take in my face, my hair.

"Thought you could escape me? Thought you could embarrass me? You should have known I would find you. So help me, you had better be intact, Miss Mary Marvel. I not only have an entire tour of Germany and France booked, but I have an equally agreeable suitor ready, willing and able to implant an heir in that useless womb."

I am struck numb. Like time and space have opened to swallow me whole. "No. No. No. No."

No tears. I am beyond tears. Awe and horror at what awaits me drive all sorrow from my soul, leaving behind a numb void.

"I am afraid that shall not be possible, Lord Manners. You see, Miss Teagarden now belongs to me. Permanently." Silas has arrived, flanked by three burly workers. His white cane taps menacingly in his palm.

Father snaps his fingers and four soldiers shuffle out of the shadows, rifles raised.

"Who do you think you are? *You* are nothing. *A peasant* to be squished beneath the toe of my boot."

Silas lunges at my father and I dive and roll out of the way.

Gunfire, shouts and screams echo amidst the snap of fists pummeling jaws. The deck is chaos and I scuttle away like a crab to the deck's edge. And consider…jumping.

The pendant burns like never ever before. As if my mother calls.

249

I gasp as it *lifts* off my chest, pulling toward the crowd.

Hesitantly, I follow the pendant's pull, crawling through the battle, heeding the call of the metal towards…metal.

My father's sword clashes with Silas'. My eyes steal up to the blade. Embedded in the hilt is…my other earring.

My magnolia stands out, glistening in the night.

It all but *sings* with the proximity of the other. My stomach free-falls, but I force myself forward into the bloody fray.

Clink, clash. Slice. "Ah! You fool!"

My father drops the sword and it skids across the deck. In mid-slide it alters course, skidding to a halt at my feet.

My brother leaps before father, shielding him and resuming the fight with Silas.

I rip the chain from my neck and place the earring against the hilt.

The two glow white-hot and fuse. I wriggle, hard, with all my might and it pops from the sword. *Thunder* erupts overhead.

Lightning flashes.

I slide backwards, counting. "One, two, three."

Lightning strikes. It strikes the guest house. A huge, flaming orange blaze erupts.

The Elementi pond behind the house…

Silas whirls. I am forgotten. His one true love…is burning. "No!"

He bolts through the battle, charging toward the guest house, now completely ablaze.

Father sees me, his gaze instantly assessing my actions, falling to my fisted hands. He crawls toward me, cradling the slice in his arm. Crimson overflows it, leaving a bloody trail across the deck.

"The only way you will ever escape me...is if you follow your mother. In *death*, "he spits.

I raise my fist high and the lightning flashes again. "Five, six...*seven*." I raise my hand high, like a lightning bolt, daring it to come. As it did for George.

Let the lightning take me.

A hot white bolt strikes the water not three feet from the boat. A tiny circle of fire lights in the bay.

"I would gladly follow her anywhere," I scream, the tendons in my neck popping out with the fervor.

My strength and confidence return, emboldened by *The Elementi.*

Father lunges, clutching me, pushing my head over the deck railing. "Go to her then. Find her in the watery deep. You deserve one another."

I flail, my boots leaving the deck for a second and I push them back down. The black water waits below.

"Allegra!"

My heart lifts. Brighton's voice. High overhead?

The festive red and white stripes of the aerial balloon are a bizarre contrast against the battle below.

He throws out a rope. I try to snatch it, but father grasps my fingers.

I laugh. I know he would break them, but he needs them for music. Always for the music.

Jonesy has returned at my side. He grabs the rope and tethers it to the deck rail. The boat moves with the force as the storm wind blows against the hot air balloon.

Father wraps both arms about my chest, pinning me to the railing.

I squeeze my fist tighter around the earrings and...I blink.

A strange, swirling of clouds has begun, directly below the balloon.

The heat in my hand is unbearable, but I clap it firmly closed, picturing a branding iron in the shape of a magnolia against my skin.

Brighton sails into the dark air, almost suspended for a moment before leaping to a crouch on the deck.

One soldier, two, attack. His fist cracks one across the face and he flies backward, crumpling, instantly motionless to the deck.

The other hesitates, but slices his sword toward him. Brighton's boot connects with his wrist, snapping it instantly so that is hangs like a broken tree branch.

He falls to his knees clutching it. Jones arrives, delivering an uppercut, laying him flat.

"Jones," Brighton's voice is thick with emotion.

"*Go*! Go my friend! This isn't goodbye." He turns to deliver another punch.

But something in Brighton's expression makes me doubt.

The lightning is a constant strobe light of flashes and booms with barely a space between. Too many to count.

Brighton hauls on the rope, pulling the basket down beside us.

"Go darling, go now." His voice is eerily calm.

I don't hesitate, I scramble onto the railing and my hands find the top of the basket. With a speed as fast as the lighting, Brighton vaults into the basket, hauling me up and in, in a single movement.

Jones lets loose the rope and we rise toward the storm.

But my brother rushes the rail, reaching it at the last moment to snatch the dangling rope in the air, halting our ascent.

"Help me!" he calls as four soldiers rush to his aid.

"Go Jones. Now is the time."

Jonesy's black eyes are uncertain, but Brighton nods and he nods back...and turns and is gone. Running toward the dock.

Toward Sarah. Toward Lucy.

My brother has managed to secure the rope to the railing once again. His lithe body now slithering up the rope toward the basket.

The balloon shakes and lurches to and fro in the wind and from the weight of him putting it off balance. It tips dangerously and I cry out.

I open my hand to show Brighton The Elementi.

They glow like the white in his father's eyes. He quickly plucks them from my palm to gently place them in my ears.

The glowering sky shifts, the odd churning dropping into the bay below.

His eye light with revelation. "Of course."

"What, I don't understand." Images flick across the small, tight circle in the water below.

"The earrings. They are forged with the highest amount of the element."

I stare into the water. My brother moves up; ten feet, six feet, four feet away.

"Your mother. Your dear mother understood what I could not. With great concentrations, the lightning and voltage are far less important. The element forms the doors. With this much in one place, you may open a door in any water, no matter how trace the amount of the element. She knew. She had these made for you, intending to take you with her. So you could always find your way home. To her."

I chew my lip, working through it. "These were her fail safe. To draw me to her, or to a better life, a different life, if something went wrong."

He nods, vigorously. Triumphantly.

He gestures below.

The balloon lurches hard as my brother's hands appear on the basket's rim.

I swallow and nod to the churning, whirl of water and wind below. "A door?"

"A door. Do not be afraid my love. I shall be with you."

The earrings burn as if answering my question.

Brighton pulls off a sandbag, wrapping one first about his leg, then one about mine. We shall…sink beneath the waves. Very, very quickly.

Thunder and lightning call above.

He hoists me to stand on the baskets edge as I clutch the rope. He does the same.

My father catches sight of us. "You cannot!" He screams.

He believes we shall take our lives, like the Romeo's and Juliet's before us.

My brother falls into the basket on the opposite side.

Brighton takes my hand. "Now, my love."

I clasp it and we leap.

For a moment, we free-fall and all time halts.

The sandbags hurtle before us, hitting the water with a *splaaash*.

For a moment my life whizzes past in music, through the frolic of childhood and quickly to the present requiem of impending death.

But it mourns for the passing of *this* life.

Surely, if we drown, if the door does not open—there is elsewhere, something better. Something more to come.

Where Elementi's are prevalent as the flowers of this earth.

We hit the water. The cold. But Brighton's hand and the element are both warm against my skin. We sink, farther and faster.

Above the surface of the water, the lightning stops. The winds cease.

A gentle breeze blows across the bay as the balloon takes flight in a billowing festive red and white puff, blowing across Fire Isle.

I feel the pressure. The cold. And keep my eyes on Brighton as my chest begins to constrict.

EPILOGUE

Am I dead?

Blackness. The all-consuming pressure of the sea against every bit of my body. My lungs next to bursting.

The creaking of sunken ships.

The far off call of whales, lamenting to one another, humming throughout my deadened skull.

Water. Brighton. The balloon.

I feel a pressure grip my fingers and I slowly turn to see Brighton's pinched, pale face for a second only, because with his free hand he is struggling madly toward the surface, his massive strength propelling him upward as if he had fins.

But still, I am holding him down. I must have lost consciousness—but he held fast to me, risking his own life to carry me through.

I release his hand and he halts, fear heightening his expression—but seeing I now swim of my own accord, he resumes his furious kicking toward the light. Our salvation.

Colors like I have never seen cast across the

surface above. I would weep at their beauty were I not below water.

Voices. Voices call, filtered and murmured and altered by the layers of water which blanket us.

"*Brighton!*"

Sloshing through the shallows. Boots, both masculine and feminine. Three pair.

The light is brighter, air is very close. I command my legs to kick harder.

Brighton reaches down and grasps my hand, giving me a final lift and shoving me upward.

The water parts, breaking across my face and I instantly relish the sun against my cheeks and suck in a five second *gasp.*

Nothing has ever felt so good. I cough and sputter and blink, trying to see.

I blink and the world, this world, comes into view. Everything looks the same, but different—more vivid, more beautiful, more perfect.

"Brighton! Oh thank Providence, Brighton!" The voice is sonorous, deep, like the sound of my cello.

Brighton has reached the shallows and stands on shaky legs. "G-George?"

His voice is full of pain and wonder.

His younger brother rushes forward, grasping him in a bear-hug. "I cannot believe you are here. I never thought I would be so fortunate twice."

"G-George?" Is all Brighton can muster.

His diction is perfect, no trace of confusion or abnormal muscle tone exists. He looks like the most perfect specimen of mankind I have ever seen.

"George. Oh, Georgie." Brighton is weeping. Weeping like a small boy.

"Allegra."

My head turns, slowly. Like time has frozen.

I know the voice, but I can scarcely believe. Scarcely hope.

"Momma?" My heart bursts apart in my chest and I rush through the shallows.

She runs toward me, looking ten years younger.

I drop to my knees and cling to her wet skirts and howl into them as I feel her hands smooth the top of my head. "Shh. Shh, my darling."

"Am I really here?" I feel Brighton's hand reach for mine, and I grasp it tightly.

Momma fingers the earrings and smiles.

"You found your way home."

Author's Notes

The Multiverse Concept.
From Wikipedia:
A place where we, our other selves, inhabit.

The **multiverse** (or **meta-universe**) is the hypothetical set of multiple possible universes (including the historical universe we consistently experience) that together comprise everything that exists and can exist: the entirety of space, time, matter, and energy as well as the physical laws and constants that describe them. The term was coined in 1895 by the American philosopher and psychologist William James. The various universes within the multiverse are sometimes called parallel universes.

The structure of the multiverse, the nature of each universe within it and the relationship between the various constituent universes, depend on the specific multiverse hypothesis considered. Multiple universes have been hypothesized in cosmology, physics, astronomy, religion, philosophy, transpersonal psychology and fiction, particularly in science fiction and fantasy. In these contexts, parallel universes are also called "alternative universes", "quantum universes", "interpenetrating dimensions", "parallel dimensions", "parallel worlds", "alternative realities", "alternative timelines", and "dimensional planes," among others.

TITLES BY BRYNN CHAPMAN

BONESEEKER (BOOK ONE)
THE BRIDE OF BLACKBEARD
WHERE BLUEBIRDS FLY (BOOK ONE)
REQUIEM RED (BOOK TWO)
PROJECT MENDEL

TITLES AS R. R. SMYTHE

INTO THE WOODS
HEART MURMURS

ABOUT THE AUTHOR

Image:Author.png

Born and raised in western Pennsylvania, Brynn Chapman is the daughter of two teachers. Her writing reflects her passions: science, history and love—not necessarily in that order. In real life, the geek gene runs strong in her family, as does the Asperger's syndrome. Her writing reflects her experience as a pediatric therapist and her interactions with society's downtrodden. In fiction, she's a strong believer in underdogs and happily-ever-afters. She also writes non-fiction and lectures on the subjects of autism and sensory integration and is a medical contributor to online journal The Age of Autism.

Connect with the Author: Website | Twitter | Facebook | Goodreads

Sign up for her newsletter for new release information at her website.

Brynn's Amazon Page with links to her titles:

THE VIOLET HOUR